# L.O.V.E

—————————

## LOYALTY.OVER.VALUES.EVERYTHING

## PAPERBOI

*My Dedication*

*I won't make this too long. Too excited, and in a rush for you to get started with my very 1st page turner, published, masterpiece! Sorry For The Wait!*

*However, it would not be right and exact if I did not thank the Man (God) upstairs first! Cause without him none of this would ever be possible. So Thank U Lord!!! And of course, Momma Gwen, my Grandmother (R.I.P) I know you are looking down on this world screaming and hollering "That's my baby!!" Don't worry Momma this For You!!! This is also for my Mother-in-law, who without a doubt has been The Best You Can Ever Ask for in a Mother-In-Law. Factzzz!! And of course her lovely daughter, my future Wife, My Ever-Lasting Angel!! Babe without you, you know this would have never been possible. When everything seemed so dark, and life for me felt like the end was near, you kept that light there and reminded me every day of our 16 years that, not only are we meant to be, but our Success Is Too!! I Love you Till Da Sun Burn Out!! And what would l be without Our children(All 8 of them) And our grandbabies!!! And Mia, damn, words cannot even explain my deepest gratitude and condolence to you and your family for yall loss this year. Through giving birth to a handsome little fella, and all that has been going on this year, you still manage to believe in my hard work and talent and help with a huge percentage of this project!! Thank you!!!*

*And Last But Not Least.... All The Real MF's That Really Got My Back And Believe In Me!!! And Of Course You, The Readers!!! LET'S GO!!!*

# PROLOGUE

Latasha swayed her 5'7" (36-26-46) frame through the hallway of her Bays Water two-family home located in Far Rockaway, NY. She shared the home with her husband, Shawn Williams, also known as Swift and their twin daughters Raquel and Rachel.

On this cold December day, Latasha was making her way to the kitchen to prepare a special dinner for two. Swift loved her cooking. Swift was in their bedroom preparing to run a quick errand.

"Shawn, I'm not playing with you, you better be just an hour." Latasha yelled over her shoulder.

Swift came stepping out the bedroom.

"All I know is, you better be in that same outfit when I get back into this house."

Latasha wore a pair of pink sheer boy shorts with a matching t-shirt from Victoria Secret.

"Yeah, whatever Shawn, just know the girls are staying at Veronicas house tonight. I told them we were going out."

"Okay ma, I heard you. Just give me an hour, hour and a half tops" Swift pleaded as he walked up behind her and kissed her neck.

"Mmmh, don't start nothing you're not willing to finish" Latasha moaned while tilting her head back on Swift's 6'2" frame.

Being shorter, her head rested on his chest.

"Don't worry ma, I'm going to drop something off to my boy and I'll be right back."

Swift hated having to leave his wife of two years and the woman he had been with half of his life, at a time like this. They hadn't had a night to themselves in over a month.

However, he promised he would get at his man Nitty. Nitty was doing ok for himself out in Red Fern. Swift did not want to leave his people out to dry.

Swift had no idea that Latasha would want to spend this Saturday together. When she suggested it, he could not decline knowing how long it had been since they had alone time.

Swift reminded her what had to be done with his man, reassuring her that was it for the day. Swift would have someone else do it, but he and Nitty had this thing where they would deal with each other personally. No third parties involved.

Latasha walked swift to the door. "Ill be waiting baby. I love you!"

Latasha said as their lips touched for a passionate kiss.

Swift replied, "I love you more".

As he stepped through the door to their three-car garage, he decided to take Latasha's new 2008 Lexus 430. Swift was about five minutes away from his destination, so he called Nitty on his cellphone. After two rings, Nitty picked up.

"If it isn't Mr. Far Rock himself. What it do bro?"

"Ain't shit Nitty. I'm on my way to you right now. Where is it that you would like to meet?" Swift responded.

"Dam Swift, right now I'm in Brooklyn, at my baby mother crib. Some shit is happening out here right now."

"Well I guess you'll get this tomorrow or something" Swift said.

"Hold up Swift, I got some people I need to see out here. How about you meet me near Downtown Brooklyn? You know, by the little mall type thing they built out there." Nitty asked.

" Listen doggy, I'm not even supposed to be out here today."

"I could dig that, but come on Swift, this is Nitty asking. I'll even throw a few more attacks your way for the extra gas." Nitty said.

They both had a laugh before Swift Agreed.

Swift went along with the plan because not only was Nitty his man, but he also needed him out of the way for a week or two.

Swift was trying to be mindful being that he told Latasha an hour or an hour and thirty. Swift made his way through Red Fern and hopped on the BQE. Seeing though as it was after 6pm and the fact that it was cold, there seemed to be no one outside other than some early Christmas stragglers.

Swift pulled in a side block facing Fulton Street, the main strip. He called Nitty and gave him his location. Nitty said he was 15 minutes away. They both hung up.

Swift decided to smoke a cigarette, so he rolled down the window knowing that Latasha hated the smell of them.

As Rick Ross' "Maybach Music" drowned Swifts' thoughts, his phone rang. He looked down at the phone on the 3rd ring while he was flicking the ashes from his Newport.

While answering his phone, he noticed a figure creeping up towards the driver side door.

As he reached for his 40 Glock that sat in the passenger seat, he realized he was a second too late.

The hooded figure held a 357 magnum to Swifts head. It did not take long for the unidentified figure to see that Swift was reaching before squeezing 2 shots into Swifts head.

Swift was dead before the first bullet exited his forehead. His brains splattered all over the windshield. A Black on black '07 G430 Lexus truck pulled up at a screeching halt besides Swifts parked car.

One man emerged from the back seat with a hoody on. The

masked man and Swift's shooter went through the trunk of the car, the back seat and the glove compartment.

The shooter spoke first.

"I got the work"

"Aight, then we good. Let's go" his partner said.

"How much is in there?" the getaway driver asked.

"I don't know, but we can count later." The shooter said while making his way to the truck.

Take some out and leave it in the truck" the driver ordered. The shooter was puzzled at this point. He knew better than to ask questions. He didn't really give two shits anyway. He dug in the Gucci bag and pulled out one square block of coke.

He jumped in the back of the truck, but not before the driver asked "I know you two niggas left his gun in his car, right?"

The shooter passed Swifts' Glock 40 to the driver. The driver wiped it down and threw it back into Swifts' car as he drove off.

# CHAPTER 1

The year was 2009 and there were only a few weeks left, until the first day of school.

The twins, Raquel, and Racheal would be entering their junior year come September. They both could not wait till the following year, being that they would be graduating.

On this nice August day, the twins and their best friend Veronica were doing some last second shopping on Mott Avenue.

Racheal, Nicknamed Rah Rah, wore her hair in a golden-brown Rihanna style cut that matched her skin complexion. On her slim (34-24-40) but curvaceous frame, she wore a pair of Burberry capris and some opened toe Dior sandals that matched her top.

"Rah Rah, what's wrong with you?" Veronica asked.

Veronica had her hair in a ponytail like always. She wore a pair of buffalo jean shorts with a pair of 95 Airmax and a neon green Lacoste shirt.

"VVS, my stomach is killing me." Rah Rah answered.

They called Veronica, VVS because they were the initials to her government name.

"That's because the heifer's period is coming down" Raquel stated.

Raquel was the oldest of the twins by a whole two minutes. The way she acted, you would have thought she had Racheal by two years.

Raquel was wearing a pair of Gucci sandals, and the same capris her sister wore with a spaghetti strap blouse. She wore her hair in a doobie.

"And how would you know?" Rah Rah Asked

"Because you get yours as soon as mines go away. And it's been like that since we started our periods."

"Well I'm ready to go home" Rah Rah whined.

They walked into KFC after VVS had expressed her hunger. There were a group of guys sitting down having a bite to eat as they walked in.

There were other people in the store, but this group was the loudest.

Veronica made her way to the cash register with the twins by her side.

One of the fellas got up from where he sat to approach the ladies.

"Which one of you will be the lucky one to join Black the Don tonight at the movies?" the young kid asked.

They all looked at him, then all looked at each other, then busted out laughing.

"See, can't be nice to you pretty bitches. Yall don't know how to fucking act!" said the kid named Black.

VVS being the loud one and always ready to fight, said something first.

"Who the fuck you calling bitches? Matter of fact don't answer that. Just smack a bitch if you in the company of one."

As soon as those words left her mouth, Raquel walked up to the boy and smacked the black off him. The boy was so shocked at what just happened, that it took a few seconds to register.

When it finally did, he tried to grab Raquel by her neck and punch her in the face.

Before he could land a punch, an arm had hooked his arm.

"Don't do it like that homie" a tall, brown skinned, handsome man said.

By now, all of Blacks homies were trying to diffuse the situation.

Rah Rah was now hysterical and crying. VVS held her off to the side while the tall gentleman cooled down Raquel, while the rest of the crew took Black outside.

"Shorty are you ok?" the tall gentleman asked.

"Yes, I'm fine and my name is not shorty. Its Raquel, but you can call me Rockie." Raquel said with an attitude.

"Well maybe if your hand were a closed fist, you'd have that knock out like Rocky. Maybe next time, right?" he asked.

That put a smirk on her face. As quickly as her smirk appeared, it left just as fast.

"So, can I pay for the food? Offer you ladies some money? It's not about the money Ms. Rockie. I'm a little embarrassed with my homies actions and would like to pay for his mistake."

"Oh Yeah? Well thanks, but no thanks" Rockie said.

"You know you're beautiful when your angry?"

"Yeah, you think so? It is funny that you say that because I do too. I didn't get your name."

"It's G-Money to my friends." He answered.

Just then VVS and Rah Rah were standing next to Rockie. "What up Rockie? Everything is ok, right?" VVS asked.

"Sure everything is fine now!" G-Money answered.

"I didn't ask you, I asked my sister." VVS said while turning her attention to Rockie.

"Well excuse me Sistah!" G-money said jokingly as he put one fist up in the air. He continued "Nah, but seriously ladies. I would like to apologize to the three of you personally for my homie's childish ways. If there is anything I can do, feel free to call and ask for the favor anytime".

With all that said and done, he said his goodbyes and walked out the store.

"Girl, I won't lie, that nigga was fine as hell." VVS shouted.

They sat in Veronicas room, munching down on their KFC, and discussing today's events.

"He was alright" Rah Rah said.

"Please Rah Rah, you were seeing him through teary eyes, with your crying ass" Rockie said.

They all started laughing their heads off. "That is funny, but then again it's not. Ain't no telling what could've happened after you smacked that thug" said Rah Rah.

"VVS, I don't know where this girl get this scary shit from, but hopefully she'll grow out that shit.

They all began to laugh again.

"So what are you going to do Rockie?" VVS asked.

She was referring to calling G-money.

"I don't know yet. He seems like a cool dude, that has his boys on smash. You know that's a turn on for me."

"There you go, trynna find somebody like daddy" blurted out Rah Rah.

They all got quiet thinking about the Twins father who was murdered last year.

"Why would you bring up daddy for? He has nothing to do with my preference in men." Rockie said upset.

"Yall, don't start this because yall know what it leads to. Rah Rah, if she wants a little thug in her life, then so be it. This shouldn't have nothing to do with Uncle Swift, may he rest in peace!" VVS stated.

"Yeah, maybe if you got a gangsta in your life, you'd straighten up with your soft ass." Rockie shouted.

"Well you know daddy would not want you with no hoodlum. And mommy wouldn't accept it either."

"Listen Rah Rah, just so you know, I don't need no man! Mommy and daddy taught me all I need to know about being independent. However, if I choose to deal with someone of daddy's caliber, then so be it."

The girls went back and forth for over an hour thinking back to how Swift used to treat his family.

Lil Wayne's "A Milly" song broke their conversation. The song came from Veronicas phone.

"Hello?" she answered on the second ring.

"Don't be acting like you don't know who you're speaking to" the male voice said on the other line.

She knew it was her boyfriend Dro but acted as if she had an attitude. Veronica knew this would get him to do just about anything she wanted.

" I don't know if you got my calls, but I called you over three times today." Veronica whined.

"I was on the road baby, so I might've had no reception. You know I miss you and I was calling to see if I could come and check you?' Dro asked.

Veronica put him on hold while she discussed her plans with the twins. She picked back up.

"Alright, you can come through. Ima call the twins a cab in a few."

"Ight cool" Dro responded before hanging up.

After hanging up with Dro, Veronica called the twins a cab.

They gathered their things preparing to head downstairs. Veronica walked them down.

"You bitches better not try to leave a mess in my room."

The twins looked at her like she had three heads. Raquel could not keep quiet.

"This your room, that you're kicking us out of for some punk ass nigga. Since its your man and your room, you clean it bitch." Rockie said with emphasis.

The twins gave each other a high give as they stepped out of Veronicas room laughing.

The trio found their way downstairs in front of the Co-op building Veronica lived in.

Before they could sit their shopping bags down, a 2008 Jeep commander with 22-inch rims, pulled up to the building.

"My stank ass sisters, there's yall cab" Veronica said with a smile on her face.

"Get to getting it ladies"

The twins grabbed their bags and gave Veronica kisses on both sides of her face.

"Bitch don't think this doesn't get written in our diary" Raquel stated.

"Yeah, you will be paid back for this." Racheal blurted out.

"Shut up Rah Rah, you have to get a man before you could try to pull this off."

They all laughed as the twins walked to the jeep. The twins hopped in the jeep with the promise to call when they got home.

# CHAPTER
## 2

On the twin's way home, Racheal asked Raquel questions about today's events and whether they should tell their uncle Fresh about it. For security reasons, Racheal felt as if they should let him know. Since their father was killed, she was still paranoid. Their uncle informed their mother that their fathers' killer could not harm any of them. Racheal remembered uncle Fresh Stating "The man who had his hand in having Swift killed, is no longer breathing." She stood in her father's work office, which stood across from her parent's bedroom. Racheal was eavesdropping on their conversation. Seeing that Rachel could never forget that night, she felt as if someone were still out there that wanted her family dead. Racheal always thought about seeing her father's killer in person. She was always curious as to what they looked like because her dreams were not always as clear. Racheal was as scared of the lifestyle her and her family lived, then a white girl in a scary movie. That is the reason why she promised her parents she would become the best psychiatrist to ever do the job. That way, she figured she would never have to deal with the street life. Right now though, it seemed like it was a fight to get there alive. Racheal was now being broken out of her trance. "Rah, Rah......Rah Rah!"

Raquel screamed over the sounds of Swizz Beatz song "Money in the Bank" "Damn Rockie, what happened?" Racheal whined. "You asked me a question then just..." Raquel paused. "Beamed up to Pluto somewhere. I think you better try to get a psychiatrist instead of trying to become one for real Racheal." Right then, Racheal knew Raquel was serious. She almost never called her by her real name. Raquel continued. "I know what's been on your mind, but you have to trust me twin. I will never let anything happen to us. With the way I have my foot on uncle Fresh's neck, he'll be extra careful with our lives." As she spoke those last words, they both had to laugh. The African cab driver pulled up to the home the twins shared with their mother. Before coming to a complete stop, the driver spoke in his best English accent. "Relax ladies, I'll get your bags and the door." "Ahh, that's so nice of you pa-pi" everyone in the truck began laughing. When the African man came to a complete stop, he said. "I will surely take care of the beautiful mamitas" with a Rico Suave accent. The driver lifted his crispy blue yankee fitted in a gentleman's manner. While he jumped his 5'8", 160-pound frame out the truck to head to the trunk, Rockie could not help but to think out loud. " I like the Africans attitude." As soon as she said it, she knew she sparked a fuse in her twin. "Don't tell me you think he's cute. Besides, how could you even look at a cab driver as nice? They must be nice to get their money. We can see right through that." Rah Rah put up the peace sign and pointed to her eyes and then Raquel's eyes. "You're absolutely right and I see right through it, he has a little humor in him too. That's what starts a beautiful friendship." Rockie shot back. They were interrupted by the cab driver opening the back door. "I hope you beautiful ladies had a nice ride enjoy the rest of your day" he said while holding the door with one hand and bags in the other. Rocky got out, then helped her sister out. She then reached into her Gucci bag that matched her sandals and pulled out a $20 bill. She passed it to the cab driver, who took it and began going in his bootleg Roc and Republic jeans pocket. Being that the ride was only ten dollars, the cab driver was getting Rockies change. Once she noticed she said "There's no need for change, it yours. Kay papi?" Rockie said with a wink. "It's ok sweetheart, I really appreciate it" the cab driver said while passing her a ten-dollar bill back. All she could do was look at Rah Rah with the "I told you so" face. Rockie took the money and asked did he have a card. She wanted one just in case she needed a cab again. The driver passed a black business card with silver glittered writing on it. The twins began strutting towards their home. The cab driver lifted his hat once more. "Again, have a good day ladies." When the twins walked into their home, the aroma from their mother's dinner, smothered their noses. "Something smells real scrumptious, Ma, you at it again?" Rockie asked their mother. It was Latasha's second big dinner this month. She only made dinner when thinking about her husband, the twins' father. "Mommy its ok, you're not the only one that's been thinking about daddy" Rah Rah said. She walked over to her mother after dropping her bags in the living room. Rah Rah hugged her mother tight while Rockie followed right behind her. "Ma, you and Rah Rah are driving daddy crazy up there. He is looking down saying to himself 'I know I taught my ladies to be stronger than they're acting.' Ma, we have to hold it down like daddy expects of us." "Raquel, baby, this is why your father nicknamed you 'Rockie', you were always so rough and so hard. Meanwhile, Racheal was the opposite. So soft and so sweet. She took after me and of course, you took after your father. I am happy you are so strong and taking things so easy. Although I am always thinking about your father, today I decided to make dinner for uncle Fresh's Birthday. I see his favorite nieces forgot" "First of all ma, we are his only nieces and second......we forgot Uncle Fresh's birthday." Rockie said in a whining tone. "We have to go back out to get uncle Fresh a gift. Mommy, what time will he be getting here?" Rah Rah asked. "Well I just spoke to him about 15 minutes ago. He said he will be by in another hour or two." Rockie went to grab the cordless phone so that she could call the African cab driver back. While she did this,

Rah Rah went to the bathroom and changed into something more comfortable. "Rah Rah you'll have to hurry because papi will be here in 15 minutes." Rockie said while laughing. "You're so silly Rockie." Rah Rah screamed from upstairs. They got themselves together and was out the door to get Fresh a birthday gift. Meanwhile across town, Fresh had his 220-pound frame leaning on his new 2010 Jaguar XJ as he was talking on his cell phone. He stood double parked on the corner of Hassock street, where a few of his peoples crowded the corner store. "Big homie, I appreciate your assistance with that situation, and I would love to repay you in some sort of way. I won't take no for an answer." Fresh spoke through his cell phone. He was speaking to the connect he had been dealing with ever since Swift introduced them 3 years ago. Now he dealt with him on a more personal level due to Swifts death last year. "Well you know, I'll do anything so my boy rest in peace and make sure his ladies are straight. Ya dig? So repaying me won't be necessary." The connect replied. "I can dig it, you'll be repaid somehow. Anyhow, I'll be ready to get up with you this week, how does that sound?" "Sounds like a plan. Right now, enjoy your birthday dinner with the ladies. Give them my unconditional love." Fresh hung up after agreeing to seeing him this week and giving his love to the twins and Latasha. "Yo fresh, come get another glass of this Henny bro." Games said. Games was Fresh's lieutenant and little man. "Yeah I'll take another glass but this one is to go. You know I got Latasha and the twins waiting on me." "Aight, but don't act like today ain't your b-day. Shit, you could have a bottle or two with the peoples" Games said in a frustrated tone. "Yo G, we got to keep this mother fucking block popping!" with that said, he grabbed him another cup and jumped in his Jag. Before pulling off, he checked himself in the mirror, took his drink back then was ready to go.

# CHAPTER

## 3

Jumping out of his all black 2008 745i, G-money with his 6-foot slim frame, gave dap to the fellas on the corner. G-money considered himself to be a pretty boy, who had a very dangerous side when it came to the streets. On this particular day, everything seemed to be ok. Leaving his car double parked, he approached a small crowd of dudes playing dice. G-money wore a copper Pelle Pelle leather with a black t-shirt under. On his feet he rocked a pair of copper and black Foamposite sneakers, and he wore a pair of black denim Red Monkey jeans. "I hope my paper good around here." G-money said out loud to no one in particular. The short chubby dude who was rolling the dice spoke. "Now you know that black card money is always good in my bank." He stood up and shook the dice over his head. "Scream a number. That's the only way I'll be able to spend look alikes around here" "Well how about we forget a number and you just stop the bank? And to make things more interesting, lets bet a light hundred you don't throw those trips you're bragging about." G-money said. The few that crowded around said their "Oohs and Ahhs". The chubby dude then told everyone that had a bet, they no longer had a bet and it was because G-money stopped it. "Oh G-money, no bet to the trips." He then rolled the dice. The dice hit the wall, one came up 5, the other was a 4. The last kept rolling for a second longer before landing on another 4. "That's a fever for the $1,200 that sits in the bank. Now bet that $100 you don't beat the 5." G-money picked up the dice and with a sly grin said "Bet" G-money began shaking the dice when his phone went off. He paused then switched hands to answer the call. When he picked up on the second ring, a soft voice spoke. "Hello, may I speak to G-money?" "Speaking. Who's this?" G-money put his finger up to the chubby kid to let him know to give him a minute. "You must have a few ladies that call you, huh?" The soft voice asked. Now that G-money knew who it was for sure, he went back into mack mode. " Well to be honest miss lady, I had a few ladies calling until this beautiful voice called" he made sure to put emphasis on "Had". "So do I call you Rockie, or is this Raquel I'm speaking with?" "Tell you what mack daddy, whatever you like, I love." Rockie replied. G-money almost forgot he was in a dice game, he told Rockie to hold on for a second. He held the phone in his right hand and with his left, he threw the dice to the wall with no care in the world. But to his surprise, the numbers 4,5,6 popped up on the dice. The crowd began talking shit and the chubby dude could not believe it. He peeled of $1,300 dollars and passed it to G-money. "Good looking Chubb's, you just paid me to take my future out." G-money then put the phone back to his ear. "So when are you taking your future out?" Rockie asked. "Damn, you heard that? You wasn't supposed to hear all that." "Well are you going to answer my question or go around it G-money?" "If you must know, with this free money I just won, I was hoping I could take you out." "Oh, so I'm your future?" "Only if you want to be ma." G-money and Rockie talked for over an hour while he sat in his car.

"YO GAMES, if I have to bail another one of your little mans out because of some stupid shit, you might as well recruit a whole new team. I should not have to be called on for stupidity. Then I had to cut my birthday dinner short with my loved ones for it!" Fresh was giving games a third-degree lecture while sitting in his living room watching Bloomberg Money News. Fresh liked to stay in tuned with the stock market. "Aight bro, you got it. My bad." Games said apologetically. Games continued "So what it's looking like for tonight? Are we getting up or what?" "Yeah, I'll come through later. I will ring your phone when I'm on my way." Fresh hung up from Games, still annoyed with his little cousin's actions. But Fresh knew Games was one of the most loyalist dudes he had on his team. He was young and devoted, which Fresh appreciated. That made Fresh think back to when him and Swift first met Games. It was back in 2005 when Fresh and Swift first got on. They just came back from copping their first key of coke from the Bronx. They walked into building 12-70 in the back of Red Fern with the key in a book bag. They had been hustling out of this building for over a year already. The spot was on the 3rd floor where they sold nickels and dimes. When they walked inside the building, Games and a couple of his friends were standing in the lobby smoking. "You little dudes stay making the spot hot." Fresh said in an aggravated tone. "Yo fresh, leave them little dudes alone. They just doing what they seen us do as kids" Swift said. Swift was the more understanding and relaxed of the two. Swift also took notice of Games being the head of the crew. "Yo shorty, you want to make a ten spot?" Swift asked Games. "Sure, I'm always willing to make a buck." Games was only 17 at the time but carried himself in an older manner. Swift gave Games a $50 bill and told him to pick up a few things from the store then, to bring it up to the spot. Without hesitation Games took the money and did what he was asked. Swift and Fresh walked up the stairs to their spot to cook up their work. On his way back to the store, Games noticed two masked men in the back stair-case. It looked like they were loading up their guns and whispering to one another. Games overhead a third party, who happened to be a female say, "You'll have to wait till I'm inside, it'll be easier to get ya in that way." Games knew that something was about to go down. Without a second thought, he rushed to Swift's and Fresh's spot. He tapped on the door, trying not to alert the people in the staircase. Swift came to the door, not sure if he heard it and looked through the peephole. When he saw that it was Games, he tucked is 9mm back in his waist and opened the door. Swift immediately noticed the fear on Games face. Before he could get a word out, Games lifted his pointer finger up to his lips to hush Swift. Games pushed his way into the door. "Yo shorty, what the hell is wrong with you?" Swift asked as he reached for his gun. "Sshhh! There's people out there in the staircase and I think they're about to run up in here." Swift Closed the door with the gun in hand. "And what makes you think that Shorty?" "I seen two dudes with guns and a mask on, then I heard a female say wait till she in..." Games words were cut off by knock on the door. Swift quietly pushed games to the back to warn Fresh. He looked through the peephole and just like Games said, a female Swift was familiar with was knocking. As he opened the door slowly, he pointed the gun directly at the female's head. She almost yelled until she saw Swift put his finger to his lips, telling her to keep quiet. "Don't make a sound or you'll die before anyone hears the shot." He whispered. Swift told her to come in slowly through the small crack in the door. As soon as she was inside and Swift tried closing the door, a body pushed its way in. Swift fell back squeezing the trigger of his gun at the figure and the door. Fresh was on his way out the room when he heard the commotion. With a Mac 11 in hand, he came out blazing in the direction of the door. Swift already hit the figure in the shoulder as he landed on top of him. He began to pump more shots in the figure while he rested on top of Swift. Fresh was putting more holes in the second dude that came through the door, than a polka dot Kwaman shirt. Fresh ran over to the body to make sure he was down for good. When he was sure the dude was dead, he ran into the hallway to make sure it was clear. Swift was on his feet and heading toward the back, but not before shooting the crackhead in the head as she laid on the floor crying. When he got to the back, Games was under the bed with a 380 in hand and the key of coke by his side. "Yo shorty where you at?" Swift yelled. Games came from under the bed. You could tell he was scared to death. "Come on shorty, we have to get up out of here." They rushed to the front of the apartment where they met up with Fresh. From the sounds in the streets, you could hear the sirens getting louder. The 3 of them made their way out the back door of the building and on to a side block. They ran across a small park and into another building. Fresh smiled at those days, he sure missed the hell out of Swift. That reminded him he had to give Latasha a call. He wanted to set a date for them to go out to eat. Fresh picked up his house phone and dialed a number. After the second ring, Racheal picked up. "Hello. Williams residence, Racheal speaking." That put a smile on Fresh's face, thinking of how intelligent the twins were and how proud Swift would have been. "Well excuse me Miss Racheal Williams, by any chance is Mrs. Latasha Williams in?" "Uncle Fresh, what's up?" Rah Rah asked with excitement. She then continued. "Mommy had to show some people a house in Long Island but said she'll be in shortly." "Ok. I was just calling to see how yall were doing and to see when you ladies were free for dinner. So make sure mommy calls me when she gets in." "You got it Unc" "By the way, how's Rockie doing?" "She's fine. She's upstairs getting dressed, would you like to speak to her?" "Nah, just let her know I asked about her. I have some business I need to tend to. I'll talk to y'all later, ok?" "Ok. Love you Uncle Fresh and be careful." "I love yall too and stay focused." Fresh hung up with Racheal and got up to start his day.

# CHAPTER 4

G-money and Rockie sat in his car in a McDonalds parking lot eating. G-money preferred that they went to a nice restaurant, but Rockie explained to him that it would be unnecessary. "I got a taste for some Mickey D's. I hope that doesn't bother you." She said while leaving the movie theater. So now she was enjoying chicken nuggets and French fries with Sweet and Sour sauce. While G-money enjoyed his Big Mac and he had a few of her fries. "You just wanted to share my fries so that I could feed them to you." "That too, but I don't eat a lot of fries." G-money replied with a smile. "But you could've bought a small one for yourself." "Whatever, how about you take those fries, which are a large by the way, and see if they can get you home." G-money said in a laughing manner. "Yeah right nigga, you wish you could kick me out your car. Matter fact, you get out! I'll make you walk home." G-money hit the master lock to unlock his doors. He then gave her a look and spoke. "Don't test me, I'll pass with flying colors. You don't have to kick me out, I'll just get out." "So all I got to do is just say the word and you'll go huh?" Rockie asked. "Don't think I'm going to really walk home though. I'll call one of my other V's to pick me up." She playfully punched his shoulder. "You are so stupid. We just seen transformers not Knight Rider. Who you think you is? Michael Knight?". They both now was sharing a big laugh. "Girl you are something else". G-money put the half of Big Mac he had left in the bag. "What's wrong, full all ready?" " Yeah I'm good ma. I had enough nachos and cheese anyway. I'll be shitting up a storm when I get home." "You are so nasty, I do have a little fries left and a nugget." They both shared another laugh. "So Raquel, seriously, did you enjoy yourself tonight? I mean, I know it wasn't nothing extravagant but I musk ask." "Well Glenn, you were definitely a gentleman." She said with a grin and continued. "And although I would've loved to be pampered with a shopping spree or a few days in Miami, or both, I'll never stop appreciating the little things. Plus, I love me some transformers. Transformers and roll out." Rockie said in her best Optimus Prime voice. "Well I'm glad you decided to call me. You failed to answer my question though. Why did you decide to contact me?" "I told you, It was easy. I said to myself 'the nigga handsome and his swag was on Pluto, I think I'll give him a call'." "Yeah, you're definitely too much." They continued to talk until Rockie said she was about to call her people to come and get her. This was a surprise to G-money. "Why don't I just drive you home and save you the trouble. I wouldn't want you breaking a nail by picking up the phone." "Ahhh, how sweet but I have to decline. I could never let too many people know where my family and I rest our heads. I remain loving from a distance until loyalty is visible. Loyalty Over Values Everything, my father taught me that." G-money was shocked at her choice of words, but more so impressed with how this young lady carried herself. "He must be a very wise man." "Yeah." Rockie said in a low tone. "Well, let me call my peoples." G-money let her make her phone call. They talked for about 15 minutes after her call was done. G-money learned that she called a cab. He did not want her to take a cab, but she insisted. The Jeep Commander pulled into the McDonald's parking lot right next to G-money's BMW. Rockie rolled down her window. "Ok Zoe, give me one sec." The African nodded his head. "Alright

Mr. G-money, It was nice and I wouldn't mind doing it again."
"That's nice to know. Just make sure you hit my phone when you
get in." "Alright. Just don't have me call more than once. Not only
would you know I am safe, but I'll also be safely pissed off. Then
I'll have to come back out here and get Rockie." They both laughed.
Rockie reached over and kissed him on his cheek. "Goodnight G-
money." G-money watched as her car pulled off. He sat in his truck
and thought to himself "She's the one."

# CHAPTER

## 5

Nitty's 6-foot, 190-pound frame sat behind the wheel of his Silver 2008 S550. He was accompanied by his right-hand man, Two-Face. "Yo Nitty, do you mind telling me where you're speeding to?" Nitty was now doing 80 mph dodging through traffic. "See if you was paying attention when we spoke on the phone, you would know I said it was time to meet the chink." Nitty said. "Damn you're right...shit, now I don't get to throw on my scooby doos. Those are shoes by the way. But I can smoke a J to this." "Not now you won't, especially in my new shit. Them dreads is starting to be too heavy for your little ass head." Nitty bust of laughing. Two-Face stood about 5'4 with dreads that hung a little past his shoulders. "That's what's wrong with you light skinned niggas now, yall think yall too pretty with yall shit. Two-Face said. They did this back and forth thing until they were pulling into the arsenal. It was located right off the West Side Highway in Manhattan. "Well where the hell this nigga hiding at, in a plane or something?" Two-Face spoke. "We have to actually jump on this chopper. They're going to drop us off on his yacht." "So he doing it like that, huh?" Two-Face asked. They both jumped out Nitty's car and walked past the rest of the parked vehicles. While passing the keys to the attendant, Nitty made sure to say, "Keep that safe sir, I'll make sure you're well taken care of." A man with a clipboard in his hand approached them. "Sir come with me. Mr. Wu, right?" he asked. "Correct" Nitty replied. The short guy lead them to a helicopter that was ready for takeoff. When they boarded the chopper, a bottle awaited them and two glasses. "Requested by Mr.Wu." The guy said. Nitty sat back and enjoyed his glass of Rosé. "Remember Two-Face, this is the move we've been waiting for, ya dig?" Two-Face gave Nitty a wink that said, 'You already know'. "Hope You're enjoying the scenery. It would not be fun getting there in two minutes" the pilot said. 10 minutes later, they landed on the yacht. Nitty and Two-Face were escorted by two of the most beautiful, Filipino women they ever laid eyes on. Mr. Wu awaited them with yet another bottle and cigars. He sat under a big white umbrella that covered a table for the three of them. Mr. Wu stood to his feet, nodded his head then took their hands to shake. "I'm glad you could make it on such short notice." "Not a problem Mr.Wu. Time waits for no man and you can't get an hour back." Nitty said. Mr.Wu nodded his head again. " Yes, Yes, time is antiquated. So keep it up." He waved for them to have a seat. Mr. Wu began talking once Nitty and Two-Face were fully seated. "Mr. Nitty and Two-Face, welcome on board in every aspect. I hope yall are ready because this could be dangerous. Yall do have the chance to decline my offer." He waited but received no response, so he continued. "So I guess you're ready to finish the job and become apart of this monumental moment." Nitty took a sip of his champagne then looked at Mr.Wu. "Mr.Wu, as you know, I wouldn't be here today If I wasn't prepared to go all the way. However, if you would be so kind to give me those numbers again in front of Two-Face. I want him to know how serious this is." Mr. Wu took a drag of his cigar. "Listen Nitty, for now 10 for you and 10 for me is fair. My 10 will run you the same number you pay for yours. So every time you pay for your shipment, you will receive something on top. And of course you'll pay for your own delivery." They all took in a smile.

"And what's our price on ten of those" Two-Face asked. "I was thinking a quarter of a mill should cover it, then another quarter when you come back. I know yall can handle this, yall should be thousand-aires by now" They all laughed out loud. Their laugh was interrupted by Nittys cell phone. Nitty looked at Mr.Wu , then looked at his phone. Raising his head back up he said, "Excuse me Mr. Wu, I have to take this." Nitty got up to his feet and stepped to the side. "Hello?" "Yo Nitty, what it look like?" Fresh asked. "Is it my time?" Nitty asked. "You already know. You can pick that up in the morning at the OV spot." "Aight, that'll work. Yo Fresh, when will we go out for a drink or two? It's been a while since we chopped it up and threw some spread in the air." "Well you know I'm just getting things back together. Nitty, to be honest bro, shit still ain't where it supposed to be. But do not worry, we'll get up and kick it about all that and then some." "Aight then, I'll just hit ya phone, when everything is green. Nitty said. When he hung up with Fresh, he walked back to his seat. Before he could sit down Mr.Wu spoke. "Is everything ok Nitty?" "It's our half ass problem, but I'm putting things together as we speak. I guess everything will be green after the holidays." "So I should be hearing from you in a few weeks?" Mr. Wu asked. "Definitely." Nitty replied. They spoke on other business ventures over lunch. Mr. Wu had his chef prepare something special for the fellas.

# CHAPTER 6

It was two weeks before Christmas, to be exact it was December 13th. The same day the twin's father was killed. Rah Rah was not taking her father's first year of death to good. She found her way upstairs, away from the crowd. Her hazel eyes stared out the window as her golden complexion glared from the sun that was now setting. The little mascara she wore, fell down her cheeks. "God, I know they say don't question you, but why?" Rah Rah said out loud to the loneliness of her heart. "I know you will keep him safe now" Rah Rah continued. A light knock at the door startled Rah Rah. Her Sisters voice slowly brought her back. "Twin...Twin, it's okay sis." Rockie walked in and hugged her from behind. Neither of them had to speak a word, Rockie's presence spoke volumes. They knew all they had was each other. Rockie broke their silence. "Now go fix that face of yours and work that Dior dress." she said jokingly. "You're so silly Rockie." Rah Rah's black shoulder cut, Dior dress was as tight as a glove on her 34-26-40 frame. "Yeah, you're right. I am working it and daddy's going to kill me twice when I get there with him. Then we have all this company and I have the nerve." With a spin to show off her curves in the same dress, Rockie said "Well daddy would want us to look good....don't you think?". Their conversation was interrupted. "There you hoochies go. I knew yall be in here hiding for a moment." "Somebody still hasn't learned how to knock" Rockie said. "Oh shut up and give me a group hug." Veronica shot back as she walked over to them with her arms open. In her heels Veronica stood 6 feet tall, but the twins still towered over her. "Aight, that's enough, you messing up my dress with your short ass." Rockie said. They made it back downstairs, where family and friends walked around with drinks and plates. Most of the guest were engaging in some sort of conversation about Swift. Swift's mother flew in from Atlanta to be with her daughter in law and grandbabies. His older sister managed to stop by. It was beyond packed at this point. Swift's mother and Fresh were making jokes about how Swift would react if he saw all these people in his house." "He would have a heart attack ma. He never wanted anyone in his house besides you. I always wondered why he built that guest room or even the Movie Room, if he wanted no one in it." Fresh was saying. Ms. Williams, who never called them by their street names said "Jamel, I just can't believe how many people showed up to his grave site today. Its too overwhelming how my only son was loved by so many people, only to die the way he did." Fresh grabbed Ms. Williams and hugged her tight as she shed a few tears. Latasha in her long silky black Versace dress with one shoulder cut out, walked her parents to where Fresh and Ms. Williams were seated. She led them to the living room. "Ma, My parents are going to keep you company for a second. I need to speak with Jamel." Latasha said to Ms. Williams. She took Fresh's' hand in hers and they walked to the front door. "What happened sis?" Fresh asked. "Do you remember Swifts people from The Bronx?" Fresh nodded his head yes. "Well they're parked outside. A Maybach and a Range Rover on my lawn. Oh yeah, Tyrick is here as well." "So they're here to pay their respects, right?" "Yeah, they called me and told me come outside because they couldn't stay too long." "Ok. So you need a little security huh?" Fresh asked in a laughing tone. "You're not funny. Anyhow, you know I'm still a little nervous with these people." "Don't be sis. You are ok right now. I can bet my right arm on it. They are with us for real. Now go on and holla at them, Ill be right here. Latasha opened the door to the house and stepped out. She walked towards the parked vehicles and a well-dressed man stepped out of the Maybach. "Mrs. Williams?" the man asked. She continued to walk towards him with her hand extended. He kissed the back of her hand. "You have my personal condolences. Excuse me, where are my manners? I'm Hots." Latasha shook her head with understanding. Hots helped her get into the back of the Maybach, where Tyrick sat with a drink in his hand. When Latasha sat down, she put a smile on her face. She remembered when Ty was still playing in college, but now he was on his way to the NBA. "How are you Latasha?"

"I'm good Ty. It's tough but I'm holding it down." "And how are the twins?" "They hanging in there. Being the best supporters possible." Ty passed her a glass while she spoke. "I'm so proud of you, not to get off topic. I know Shawn is looking down on you with a big smile." "Thanks a lot Latasha. That is why I am here and will be here until I am sitting with him. He kept me in check with the school thing. I would never let him down. I will always be there if you and the twins need me in any way. I also brought a little some-thing to leave with yall. Ty picked up 3 envelopes with names written on them. He passed them to Latasha. "These are for you and the girls. I know Christmas and stuff is coming up. The girls are getting ready for their last year and college, so I know how it can be". "You know you don't have to do this Ty. " Latasha said. "Oh, but I do. I would not be who I am if I did not. Your husband's loyalty meant everything to me." "Well thank you so much! And tell Ebony and lil Ty congratulations on their husband and fathers draft pick." "Yes, I'll let them know. By the way, I'm having a New Years party. I'll be giving yall a call, ya have to come through and represent." They said their goodbyes and promised to call as soon as the time was right. When Latasha was walking back towards the house, the twins were standing at the door. "Mommy, who was that?" Rah Rah asked. "Damn girl, you're nosey. For your information that was a friend of your fathers, his name is Tyrick." "That's who daddy used to talk about. He was going to become an NBA player, right?" "Yeah and like always, your father was right. Ty will be playing NBA basketball next year. By the way, these are for yall. They're from Ty. She passed the girls their envelopes. The twins took the envelopes in their hands. "This is a lot of bread." Rockie said with excitement. "Yeah, I'll be at the mall in the A.M. Rah Rah said. "Well, we should get back inside and tend to all these people. I want to get everyone into the living and dining rooms, so I can say my prayer and thank everyone for coming out. Latasha and the twins got everyone together as she planned.

# CHAPTER 7

D-nice was one of Games workers. He stood about 6'1", 195 pounds and he was light skinned with red curly hair. D-nice stood in the lobby of one of the buildings in Red Fern with his man Rob. Rob was a short dark-skinned chubby dude with waves. It was Christmas eve and D-nice and his man Rob was killing them with the crack they was selling for Games.

"Yo D-nice, we already finished an onion and its only about 7 o'clock." Rob said. "That's because I do this shit, little nigga." Just as he finished his sentence, two crack heads came strolling in the lobby. "Yo D-nice, I need play baby." The female fiend said as she stood there with her male friend. "Come on with this play shit tootsie. What'cha got there for me?" D-nice asked as he watched her pull some wrinkled bills out of her coat pocket. She started counting out loud till she got to $58. "I was hoping I could get 7 of those fat joints for this." Tootsie passed the money his way. Rob snatched the money before D-nice could even attempt to reach for it. "God damn nigga, you act like you got the slabs to give her. Anyway, I got 6 for you tootsie. Take it or leave it." "Come on D, I done spent all my money with you today, help a sister out." "I tell you what, take 3 dollars back and get you something to drink with that. Now you'll be paying $55 for the 6... Merry Christmas." Rob and D-nice started laughing as D-nice passed her 6 cracks. He told Rob to give her back 3 dollars and he did. Once the crackheads was gone, D-nice began counting the extra singles he kept in his back pocket. Rob was staring out the lobby window and saw two figures walking in their direction. " Yo D, I think these niggas Clarence and Black are walking this way." "What the fuck them niggas walking over this way for?" D-nice replied while pulling out his 9mm Beretta. "I never trusted these niggas to begin with." D-Nice continued. They both watched as Clarence and Black got closer to the building. "Yo Rob, if these niggas act stupid, word to mother my nigga, I'ma let Retta talk to them." "I can dig it. Real talk." Rob replied. "Yo D-nice, let me holla at you real quick." Black said as he and Clarence entered the building. There was always slight tension between D-nice and Black. D-nice came to Queens from Rochester, NY to stay with his aunt who resided in Ocean Ville in Far Rockaway. That is where he became close to Games, who had shit popping out there. Soon they made their way to Red Fern, another section of Far Rock, where D-nice was fucking some shorty named Tieara. The friction started between to the two because Tieara is Blacks baby mother. To top it all off,

D-nice wasn't even from Red Fern, let alone Queens. But he got money out there, as if he had lived there all his life.

D-nice and Black walked to the side where the staircase was located. D-nice was standing slightly to the side, so that Black could not see the Beretta he had behind his leg. "Yo my dude, we don't have much to talk about. But seeing as you are here, say what you need to say and keep it moving." D-nice said. "Oh word nigga?" Black asked. "Well check this shit right here, you high-yellow ass country wanksta, you and your lil fat bitch got to get the fuck up off." Before Black could finish his sentence, D-nice lifted his Beretta up to Black's head. The facial expression on Blacks face, was one of shock. He had to play it off, he could not let this country nigga punk him. So he said out loud. "Oh so now you G'd up, huh?

What'cha going to do with that lil homie?" Black asked with his chest out. Clarence was shocked at what was taking place. Even though he had his 380 Glock in his pocket, he did not want to make any sudden moves. "That's what's wrong with most of you city niggas. Yall think yall the only niggas shooting shit. Well, let the rest of them niggas up there know, an East Side Rochester nigga left you." D-nice said before squeezing a shot into Black's head. Things seemed to go in slow motion after pulling the trigger of his Beretta. D-nice then pointed his gun in Clarence's direction and squeezed the trigger. After 3 shots with only one hitting Clarence, the Beretta D-nice had jammed. Clarence had just enough time to get his 380 Glock out and squeeze a few shots in D-nice's direction. Rob and D-nice turned and ran in the staircase. But not before D-nice took a bullet in the upper back near his shoulder and Rob took one in his ass. They made it out the back exit through the staircase and into a back block. Rob had his 2008 Cherokee SRT8 parked there. Rob threw D-nice the keys and told him to drive, he could not sit his ass in no seat and drive right now. D-nice shoulder was killing him, but he knew they had to get up out of there. Once in the jeep, Rob laid down in the back seat on top of a black t-shirt. "Yo D, we got to get to a hospital, fast." "Yeah, but we cannot go to no hospital out here, its too dangerous. You have to remember, I just bodied this nigga and we had a shoot out!" "Aight, Aight! You're right. We have to go out to the Bronx. I know some people out there. Besides Brooklyn is too close. Are you sure you'll be able to make it?" Rob asked. "I guess so, I'm losing a lot of blood though." "Well just let me know and I'll take over." Rob offered. D-nice found his way to the highway with the crazy directions Rob gave him.

# CHAPTER

## 8

Latasha sat up in her bed with a glass of white wine that she brought up from her bar cabinet. It was pretty cold on this December day, but you would never know by what she was wearing. Her pink sheer nighty rested comfortably on her caramel complexion 36-26-46 frame. She took a sip of her drink as she stared up at her and Swift's wedding picture. For Christmas last year, Latasha had it blown up in portrait form and hung it up in their bedroom. "Baby I wish you were home." Latasha Whispered. She knew with her door closed and locked that she would not be disturbed. Racheal was the only one home and she was in her room on the computer. "Baby, the girls and I miss you so much. Racheal is working hard to become a psychiatrist. She is doing very well in school. As for you better half, she doing well in school for the most part. She has become curious about your lifestyle and think she is a replica of you. I am doing everything I can, in my power to see that finishes school. She is becoming a tough cookie to handle. That is why I wish you were here. I know you would have the answers or some sort of solution." Tears formed in Latasha's eyes as she continued. "You're not even here to celebrate with me. I've sold another house last week and received a nice Christmas bonus." Her tears were of joy as well as hurt. She could not help but be proud of what she accomplished. She only wished that her husband were here to share and enjoy it with her and the twins. Rah Rah was sitting at her desktop while on her laptop. She just hung up the phone with one of her school friends, Brittney. They were arranging a date for some after Christmas shopping. Rah Rah was looking at the latest coach bags and shoes, when she thought to see what her mother was up to. She made her way up the stairs and heard the sounds of jazz playing. Normally she would not have messed with her mother while she was listening to her music with the door closed. Since it had been a while since they had a one on one, Rah Rah knocked on her mother's door. She knocked softly. Latasha was brought out of her thoughts by the knock on the door. It could only be one of two people. She softly said "Come in." "Mommy, how are you? You look sad." Rah Rah asked. "I'm alright baby, I was just talking to your father while having a drink. Why? Everything ok with you?" "As long as you and Raquel are alright, I'm fine. I just figured I'd come bother you for a little since Rockie is out for the night." "Well, did I tell you that I sold the house in Long Island." Rah Rah went to get on the bed. "Mommy that's what's up! Congrats" Rah Rah said while crawling into bed with her mother. "Yes, it is. But anyway, where did your sister go? Does she know that grandma and grandad will be here tonight?" "I thought they wasn't coming till tomorrow. Rockie will be here though. She just went for a ride with a friend." Said Rah Rah. "What yall think mommy wasn't yall age? I know damn well your sister has a boyfriend. I will simply wait till she decides to share this with me. If it does not affect her schooling in no type of way, I am cool. That goes for you too Ms. Good girl." They both laughed. "Nah, not me mommy, I am the good one. Plus boys seem to nasty....ewww." She made a face as if she were about to puke. "Yeah well, that's just a stage you're going through. And you better one day bring a nice good-looking man home and not no damn woman! I know that much." "Mommy, I wouldn't take it that far. You always taking things elsewhere. You know your daughter would never take that route." "Ok, so tell me about this young fella your sister is seeing." "No....No, No. You think you're slick mommy." They began laughing again. Latasha asked Racheal to get up and go with her to the kitchen, she had a pot-roast in the oven she wanted to check on. When they got down to the kitchen, Rah Rah started helping her mother with the dinner they were preparing. They continued to talk about things that were going on in the twin's life when the cordless phone rang. Rah Rah picked up the phone that rested in the kitchen. It was the twin's grandmother. Rah Rah spoke to her for a minute before passing the phone to her mother.

CHAPTER
9

G-money ran out of the store in his red Nautica bubble coat, trying not to get to wet. The snow began to fall, but it had wasn't sticking to the ground. He walked to his car that was in the store parking lot. G-money jumped in and began to take off his coat. "So you drove all the way to Jersey to go in BERT'S for 5 minutes?" Rockie asked. She sat in the passenger seat, playing with the radio. "Yeah, pretty much." G-money replied. Rockie was going through something and did not need G-money asking questions, so she ignored his calls for almost two weeks. Today she finally answered his call. She only picked up because he was calling all day and left over 10 messages. "Cute, if I don't say so myself." She smirked inside. Once she answered, he convinced her to take a drive with him to Jersey. And here they were. "Are we heading back to Queens now?" "Why did you have somewhere else you'd like to go?" G-money asked. "Don't be a smart ass, kay." She said as she playfully punched him in the arm. "Damn, you got a solid jab there. You sure you don't want to be a boxer?" "I'm sure. I'm too much of a lady." She said in her best sexy voice. "Well you could have fooled me. My future, when are you going to tell me what's been keeping you away?" G-money asked as he made his way onto the New Jersey Turnpike. "I told you, I will. Once I am ready. Why must you pressure me?" "Excuse me Raquel, I didn't mean to upset you, ok? I have just been concerned with what has been pinching that big ole heart of yours". He reached over and poked the left side of her chest. Rockie quickly pushed his hand away. "Nigga stop trying to cop a free feel. With this nasty weather, stealing a feel can cause an accident." "Maybe I'll wait till we're not on the highway and the weather is better." G-money said with a wink. "I wouldn't do that if I were you. Stealing will get your fingers cut off. Just then, the song "Trust" by Keyshia Cole and Monica came through the speakers. "Oh, this my song right here!" she said with excitement while turning up the radio. Rockie was so into the song that she started the song over and took it from the top. They were in Queens when Rockie spoke again. "Glen, what was so important that you drove all the way out to BERT's in this weather for?" She asked. G-money pulled up on Mott avenue and parked in the first empty spot he saw. Never turning the car off, he turned the radio down some. "Listen Raquel, we been cool for a few months now and I've been wondering when I'd be able to call you mine? I have friends, but with you, I want more. Ya dig? "I understand Glen. I have never been in a relationship before. I don't know how to commit to a man." "Well all I ask of you my future, is to let me show you." He reached inside his coat pocket and pulled out a small gold and silver BERT'S bag. "You're not serious are you?" Rockie asked anxiously as she watched him pull a box out. She thought G-money was proposing and was nowhere near ready for it. "Raquel, I wont rush you into nothing you're not ready for. Just know I will be here, ready to become yours and vice versa. And to prove this, I had to get you this. He opened the box that contained a white gold Tiffany 'X & O' necklace. It read "FUTURE" and contained 2.5K VVS diamonds. "Oh my god, G-baby!" she held it with excitement. "What did you just call me?" "I think G-baby, why?" "I love the sound of it, that's why. Now, can I put this around your neck....Future?" She turned her back towards him so he could put her new necklace on. "This is beautiful, how much did it cost you?" "It doesn't matter, you're worth every penny and more. Merry Christmas!" "Thank you, Glen." She reached out and gave him a hug. After the hug, he asked her "What did you call me future?" "Oh, my bad. Thank you, G-baby. I love our nicknames for one another. Rockies phone rang, interrupting their moment. "What's up Zoe?" She asked as she picked up. "Nothing much. I'm on Mott Avenue about five cars behind you Rockie." "Ok. Thanks for being on time Zoe. I'll be with you in a second." "Cool. Just let me know when you're ready and I'll pull up beside you." "Ok." She hung up with Zoe and turned her attention back to G-money. "So your personal chauffeur is here?" G-money asked. "Yeah, remember I told you my grandparents were coming into town? They're spending the night to have Christmas dinner with us tomorrow." "That's what's up. I'm sure you'll call me when you get in, right?" "G-baby you know I will." She said while reaching out to hug and kiss him. "Are we still on after your New Years Eve party?"

G-money asked. "Of course we are." Rockie answered with a smile. G-moneys cell phone began to ring. He picked up on the second ring when he noticed the number. "Yo, what up boy?" he asked. "Um...is this G-money?" the voice asked. "Yeah, this is G-money, who is this calling from Black's phone?" "This is his daughters' mother, Tieara. I thought you should know that Black got shot about 20 minutes ago. Him and Clarence." "Aight shorty, I'ma call you back. I'm on my way to Red Fern now." G-money hung up and explained to Rockie what he was just told. She noticed his whole mood had changed and understood. Rockie told him to be careful and to handle his business. "Don't forget to call me when you're done G-baby"

"You know I will my future." He replied.

# CHAPTER 10

The aroma of Zoe's car smelled of some strong weed. Rockie turned her nose up.

"Zoe, you up in here puffing on some good shit, huh?" "Yeah, You know I got some shit right now." He reached in his pocket and pulled out a jar with a red top on it. It contained a neon green weed with white and red strings of hair growing out of it. "What is this?" Rockie asked while grabbing the jar from Zoe. "It's called Sour Diesel. I just got a nice shipment of this good shit. Its only right that I give it a test drive." He gave a quick smirk. Rockie had seen Zoe high before, but not like this. "You want to give it a try?" Zoe asked Rockie. "Now you know better than that Zoe. Just get me home safely, cuz your ass is burnt out." They both laughed as he pulled off. "I see somebody got an early Christmas present, looks nice." Zoe looked at Rockie through the rear-view mirror admiring her necklace. "Yeah, thank you. Isn't he nice?" "He's cool. Seems like he is really interested. I just want you to be careful. I know a few of his people and they say he is a dangerous man." Zoe explained. They spoke on G-money and his people the rest of the ride to Rockie's house. Zoe also mentioned how he would drive them around for hours as they would buy bud off him. In that moment Rockie knew

Zoe was hip to the game. She made a mental note of all the information she had just learned. When Zoe pulled up to her house, they said their goodbyes and she promised she would call him tomorrow. Meanwhile on the other side of Queens, G-money was talking to Tieara and his man Pusha. "So Black got shot in 12-70, huh?" he asked out loud. "And where the fuck is Clarence at?" "He in St. Johns too. Doctors said he got hit in the arm and leg." Pusha explained to him. "What the fuck were they doing shooting out with them niggas anyway? Never mind all that....Fuck it! I need the two of you to go to the hospital and see what is going on. Pusha, call me and keep me posted. I got to make a few phone calls myself." After giving Pusha a pound, they went their separate ways. G-money jumped in his car and called Nitty. Nitty didn't pick up the first two times so G-money left a message the third time." Yo check it bro, when you get this message, hit me back ASAP. Its been a Black Wall street at my place of residence. Get at me." G-money hung up his phone and decided he needed a drink. He drove to the nearest liquor store to buy him a bottle. As G-money pulled up to the liquor store he noticed a short, thick, Spanish chick named Maliah out front. Maliah was from the P.J.s and always tried to be in G-money's presence. When he got out the car and walked into the liquor store, she was all up in his face. G-money figured she would be gone by the time he came back out, but he was wrong. Maliah had the nerve to be leaning up against his car. All he could do was laugh because she would not quit. Shorty stayed trynna push up on G-money. He opened the bottle where he stood and took a swig as he began walking to his car. G-money could not help but notice how thick Maliah was looking. Her assets were still on display while wearing Tru Religion jeans and a Montcler jacket. "G-money, I don't know why you keep running from all of this. You can stop now papi." "Listen shorty, ain't nobody running from you, ya boy just a busy man, ya dig." "Well you don't look busy now." She said while twirling her hair. "I am really busy, you just cannot tell. You need to take your behind in the house before you get sick

tho." "Whatever G. Can you drop me off at least?" "Aight, get in."
he opened the passengers side door for Maliah to get in.

G-money walked around the car after closing her door and
jumped behind the wheel. From the corner of his eye,

G-money could see that Maliah had unzipped her coat. She
was wearing a tight Baby Phat spandex shirt that showed off her
size 34C cups. Her nipples were so hard that they could cut
diamonds. G-money could not help but notice the nipple ring in
her right breast. "I see you peeking. They are small but all mine.
And I have never gotten any complaints. Both are actually a hand-
ful." G-money took another swig of his henny and put the car in
drive. Maliah tried making small talk, but G-money was lost in his
thoughts. He sipped his bottle until he was a block away from the
projects. "Let me ask you something." Maliah said. "Go right
ahead." "Well. Don't take this the wrong way, but are you gay? I
mean, I've never seen you with a bitch and I haven't heard about
you fucking anything in the hood." "I don't take shit like that
personal. That just lets me know, I am doing the right thing out
here. Besides, don't nobody want none of these dirty bitches out
here." "So do you think or feel the same about me?" she asked.
"Nah ma, you alright. My head is just somewhere else, ya dig?"
"I'm pretty sure I could put your head where it needs to be." She
said while reaching for the zipper on his pants. "You ever got head
doing 160?"

She smirked and winked at G-money. Maliah licked her lips at
G-money seductively. He wanted to see if she would do it, so he
bust a U-turn. G-money headed for the highway as he thought to
himself. "If she play games, I'll leave her ass right on the highway"
She was surprised that he turned the car around. Maliah took off
her jacket and placed her hair in a ponytail. Once they were on the
highway, Maliah began to unbutton G-moneys pants. He took
another sip of his henny. "You must've thought I was playing with
you, huh?" she asked but did not wait for a response. "I'm only
doing this G-money because I've been trynna get with you for the

longest. Just know, I don't normally do this on the regular." G-money was listening but was not trynna hear all that shit. He let her pull his dick out and she started licking the head. G-money turned up the volume to one of his favorite 2pac joints, 'Gangsta Party'. Maliah loved the fact that he was listening to some gangsta shit while getting head. It made her pussy wet. Maliah took all 9 ½ inches of G-money in her mouth and deep throated. "Oh shit.... Damn girl." Was all

G-money could say. She was going in so hard, G-money almost closed his eyes and started speeding up. "Go ahead, cum for me daddy." Maliah said as she stroked his manhood that was covered with her spit and saliva. When she felt he was about to cum, she deep throated him one last time. Maliah sucked hard on the tip as she let him shoot his load in her mouth. Her freaky ass swallowed every drop. "As soon as G-money finished busting a nut, his phone rang. "Yo" he answered. "G-money its Push. Yo bro, shit is crazy over here. They saying Black fell into a coma and its not looking good. That nigga Clarence will be alright, but I have not spoken to him yet." "Aight bro. Get shorty home and take it down for the night. I'll call you in the AM, make sure you up, ya dig?" "You already know." Pusha hung up as G-money was getting off the highway and heading back to the projects. "Are you okay G-money?" Maliah asked concerned. "Nah, actually I'm a bit upset. But

I'ma get you home. Here, take this..." he dug in his pocket and pulled out some bills. G-money tried handing it to her. "Are you fucking serious? Do you think I'm some type of prostitute or back page bitch?" "It's nothing like that at all. You shouldn't walk away empty handed." "I'm good. I do not want your money cuz I sucked your dick. I wanted to do that. I want a lot, but you act like your scared of what I want and that's a relationship." "Well the truth is, I am dealing with someone right now and she is special. I don't know what I was thinking when I tested you" "Ok G-money, just put my number in your phone. If you ever change your mind, call me. I promise to be available." She said in a seductive tone. "G-money dropped Maliah off in Red Fern and was heading to Southside where he rested his head. His thoughts were on Rockie and he was in the mood to call her. G-money decided against it because it was late. "I'll make sure to call you in the A.M. my love, talk true!"

G-money changed the CD while he was stopped at a light. He popped in a mixed CD and skipped a few tracks. Plies and T-Pain's song "Shorty" started blasting through the speakers. G-money began singing the hook. "Even though I'm not your man, you're not my girl, I'ma call you my shorty."

# CHAPTER 11

It was New Years Eve and Veronica and the twins just finished buying new shoes from Saks Fifth Avenue. Veronica and Racheal sat in the back of Zoe's truck while Raquel occupied the passenger seat. "Did you hear about that kid Black? I heard he got hit up the other night." Veronica asked. "Are you talking about the kid Rockie smacked in KFC?" "Yeah, that's who she's talking about" Rockie said while turning in her seat to face Rah Rah. "It's sad, but... Oh well!" Rockie said trying to hold in her laugh. "That's not funny Rockie." Rah Rah said annoyed. "That's what a nigga get for pressing bitches like us." Veronica said. "I'm trying to tell you." Rockie added. Listening in on the ladies conversation, Zoe decided he had to put the ladies on. "Yall have to be careful out here. There is going to be a lot of gunplay in Red Fern. That kid Black has a bad team. So whoever had something to do with it, will have his fair share of problems. Just keep that in mind when you're hanging out around the way." Zoe drove to the BQE and lit up the clip he had in the ash tray. "Zoe, have I told you that you smoke too much?" Rockie asked. Before he could respond, Rockie's phone went off. She picked up on the second ring. "Hello" "Rockie, what are yall doing?" The caller asked. "Uncle Fresh, we're on our way home.

We just spent the day shoe shopping. Why, what happened?" "I just wanted to know what time yall would be ready, I wanted to send Games to come and pick yall up." "Mommy said that the Ty kid, was sending a car for us." "Oh really! I will check on that for you. Other than that, is everything ok?" "I guess so. When we see each other tonight, I would like to have a moment with you." "Is everything ok Rockie?" Fresh asked in a concerned tone. "Yes, Everything is good, I just need to speak with you about a few things." He agreed to it and they hung up. "What are you up to Rockie?" Rah Rah asked curiously. "Don't worry twin, I got something in the works. Just trust your twin." "You know she wont lead us wrong Rah Rah." Veronica butted in.

---

"YO NITTY, what are you going to do about this shit that happened in Queens? I mean, do you even know what that was all about?" Two-Face asked. They were sitting outside the Pink housing projects on the main strip, enjoying a bottle of Grey Goose. "Two-Face, I'm going to have to talk to Fresh about controlling his lil' soldiers out there. We should not have too much of a problem honestly. Far Rock will be mine in a minute." Two-Face just listened while sipping on his cup. He could not help but think of how selfish Nitty was. "What's on your mind, Two?" Nitty asked. "Nothing bro, just waiting on this big opportunity to unfold. I'm thirsty to take over Far Rock, we already have half of Brooklyn locked down." "Don't worry son, this shit about to happen in a few weeks. You know I'm just waiting for the perfect opportunity, ya dig?" Two-Face was thinking about how greasy this nigga Nitty was. But this was his mans since they were lil' dudes flipping on pissy mattresses. He knew it was a matter of time before bad luck came their way.

Two-Face quickly thought back to how Swift used to treat Nitty. Although he never dealt with him personally,

Two-Face knew Swift did not deserve the cards he was dealt. Two-Face also knew this was a dirty game, and only dirty niggas played it. The way things were going, he knew he would have to stay on point, like a #2 pencil without being broken. Cause ain't no re-sharpening in this game. His thoughts were interrupted by the passing BMW. The person inside was honking the horn. "That's that bitch" Nitty said. "Word. When she get that BMW?" Two-Face asked. "That probably belong to some nigga she fucking with. You know how these hoes do." "Yeah, well wait till I get up with her, I'ma have to press that." Two-Face pulled out the other bottle of Grey Goose and filled his cup up. When Nitty pulled out his phone, Two-Face asked him who he was calling. "Ima see what this nigga Fresh getting into tonight." He put the phone to his ear and waited for Fresh to answer. "What's good Nitty?" Fresh answered. "Aint nothing baby, just trying to see what's going on with you. You know, see what you getting into tonight." "I'm doing the family thing, ya dig? We are doing a little partying tonight. You know, something light. Why, what you getting into?" Fresh asked. "Basically the same thing. Watching the ball drop with the wife and kids is mandatory. But after that, Two-Face and I are going to this stripper party, up in the Players Club. They having something special for the New Year." Nitty explained. "That sounds like some place to be, but you know me baby, I don't do too much of the club scenes. Anyhow, when you think y'all be ready to holla at me?" "In about a week or so." They made small talk before they hung up with one another. When Nitty turned to talk to

Two-Face, Two-Face was lighting up a blunt. "I knew it wouldn't be long before you started smoking again." "You already know." He said with a smile. "Yo, did you call

G-money to see if he wanted to fuck with us tonight?"

Two-Face asked. "Nah, that nigga got ahold of some new pussy, so he's too busy chasing that. That is probably why shit getting fucked up on his end. I'ma have a talk with him about that in a day or two."

# CHAPTER

## 12

The ladies pulled up to Trump Plaza a little past 10 PM. In true Swift fashion, they had to roll out in style. The ladies pulled up in two of the finest cars that were present that night. Tonight, Rockie and VVS rode in a Black on Black 2010 62. S Maybach. While Latasha and Rah Rah rode in a Black on Black 2010 Phantom. The Williams Women knew how to make a grand entrance. A well-groomed young man helped Latasha and Rockie out of their car, while Rockie and VVS were standing by waiting. Rocky stood there on her iPhone discussing her date with G-money tonight. She wore the same Sandy-Grey Chinchilla waist coat Rah Rah wore. Instead of pants and a blouse, Rockie wore a one shoulder Louis Vuitton Cocktail dress. To accentuate her outfit, she wore 4-inch, knee high, Charcoal-Grey Jimmy Choo boots with a matching clutch bag. VVS stood close by with a dark reddish sleeveless fox with a hood. She wore a skirt with her sleeveless Marc Jacobs blouse. On her feet, she had under the knee cut, Dior boots the same color of her fox. VVS had her favorite Dior tote bag over her shoulders. Latasha exited the Phantom in a long black mink. Underneath, she was wearing a long sleeved, off white shift dress. She had the matching clutch, both were made by once of her favorite designers, Dolce & Gabbana. On her feet were a pair of ankle cut Chanel boots with 3-inch heels.

Rah Rah's Jimmy Choo boots sat 4 inches off the ground. Her designer shoes had Silver Criss cross chains that matched her bag. Her Silver-Grey dress pants and white blouse were both made by Michael Kors. The ladies turned a lot of heads once they were inside. They even had married men and women checking them out. Rockie and VVS enjoyed the attention as they walked to coat check. They gave in their coats and gave the last name "Williams" to the doorman. The place was packed but was so spacious you could not really tell. As they walked to the center of the ballroom, a Blonde white lady approached them. She was carrying a tray with a bottle and 4 champagne glasses. "This here is for you ladies, it's from Mr. Bright." The blonde said as she nodded and looked up to the male who was standing on the balcony looking their way. "Who is that?" VVS said in a sexy tone. "That there is Mr. Bright, and his wife is sitting right next to him." Said the blonde. They all grabbed their glasses as Latasha said "That's yall father's friend, Ty. Veronica, I'ma need you to cool your hot ass down." The blonde poured Nuvo into their glasses while everyone smirked. Once the blonde walked off, Latasha began. "Ok, yall be on yall best behavior and there will be no heavy drinking tonight. Do I make myself clear?" "Ma, VVS is about to be 19 and we'll be 18 in about a month or so. Give us a break." Rockie cried. "Yeah, yeah, whatever. You heard what I said. Now let us go up here to see Ty. He waved for us to come upstairs" They followed behind Latasha while a few heads turned to look in their direction.

---

FRESH AND GAMES got out of Fresh's Jaguar, looking so fresh and so clean. Fresh had neatly braided, straight back corn rolls. His Navy-Blue Armani suit was tailor fitted, complimenting his Black Armani Ostrich boots. He had to top it off with his $5,000 Tag

Hauer time piece. Games stood at 5'11", 190 pounds. He wore a pair of Black Louis Vuitton slacks with a Black V-neck Louis Vuitton sweater. Games had his Platinum Cartier Frames on, and his dreads were done neatly with them hanging down to his neck. Games loved being iced out and added his 3 ½ Carat Cartier watch and his custom-made platinum Cuban link with an iced-out Jesus piece. On his feet he wore a pair of Louis Vuitton loafers. Games comrades pulled up behind them in Games 2010 Money Green Denali with Peanut Butter interior. Dro was the driver and Ratley was in the passenger seat. They both exited the Denali wearing Hugo Boss slacks with cashmere sweaters. Dro had on a Green cashmere sweater while Ratley chose a Wheat color. Dro wore his 2 Carat diamond studs in his ear with an Arctica time piece. Ratley wore a pair of the same 2 carat diamond studs and opted to go with his Mr. Freeze time piece. They got out and followed behind Games and Fresh. As they entered the building, Fresh turned around to Dro and Ratley. "You two fools be on your best. As you can see, this is what they call a ballers convention" There were a few rappers, comedians and even a few NBA players in attendance tonight.

# CHAPTER 13

D rake's "Best I ever had" spilled through the speakers as Rockie danced closely to a tall light skin brother that stood at 6'5". VVS was dancing not too far way with a shorter brother that was rocked a bald head. They had been on the dance floor for about 15 minutes now and VVS was in the mood to grab a drink and sit back. Just as she tapped Rockie she watched Games, Dro and Ratley walking through the crowd. VVS stood there shocked for two reasons. First, she had never seen any of them dressed the way they were. Secondly, she did not think she would be bumping into them at this event. "Rockie, look who's here." VVS said in Rockies ear because the music was too loud. When Rockie looked up and saw the fellas, all she could was smile. Rockie knew that if Fresh was here, then Games and his crew would be here too. She wasted no time leaving her dance partner right where he danced, to walk up to Games and them. "Well, what a surprise." Rockie said while approaching Games. VVS could not believe Rockie had just did that. She was too bold at times and VVS hated it. "Ok, I see you Rockie. What's good besides ya beauty?" Games asked. Even though Games was like a nephew to Swift, he found the twins to be the baddest joints to come out the Rock. They were both beautiful,

but Games was more attracted to Rah Rah. She reminded him of
Rihanna. They could pass for sisters. "Why thank you Games.
Ain't nothing though, what's up with you and ya peoples, and
where's uncle Fresh at?" "He up in here, somewhere talking to
some important people. You know how he could be. Anyway,
where's Ri Ri?" Games asked as he called Rah Rah by Rihanna's
nickname. "You know we had to get VIP baby!" Rockie said while
pointing up to where her mother and Rah Rah sat. To follow suit,
VVS made her way in their direction. When Dro laid eyes on VVS,
he could not believe how sexy she looked. "What's good baby girl?"
Dro said as he opened his arms to hug her. "You look stunning." He
said in her ear while they embraced. "Thank you Dro. You're
looking real spiffy yourself." She softly kissed him on the lips. Dro
grabbed VVS by the hand. "We bout to spin off to the bar, I'll catch
up to you niggas in a minute." He said over his shoulder. Rockie
lead Games and Ratley up to where Latasha and Rah Rah were
seated. The ladies were enjoying a couple of Margaritas in the VIP
section. While walking through the crowd, they ran into Fresh and
Ty. "Are you enjoying yourself Raquel?" Ty asked Rockie when he
saw her coming his way. "Yes Ty, thanks for asking. I would like to
have a moment with you when you're not too busy." "Well I'll tell
you what, I'm about to go to the rest room really quick. How about I
meet you in your VIP section?" Ty asked. "Ok, sounds good." That
placed a big smile on Rockies face as she continued on her way.
When they got to their section, Games gave both Latasha and Rah
Rah tight hugs. He introduced Ratley to Latasha, Rah Rah already
knew him. "How are you doing Mrs. Williams?" Games asked.
"I've been fine. Thanks for asking. How are you and the family
doing?" Latasha asked back. "Everyone is fine. It's good to see you
enjoying yourself." "Yeah, well we are bringing in a New Year,
right?" Not looking for an answer, she continued. " I decided to get
out with my girls and enjoy the New Year." She grabbed her drink
and took a sip. Games ordered two bottles of Rosé and sat next to
Rah Rah as Ratley sat beside him. When Ty came upstairs, he held

a bottle of Rosé in his hand. You could tell he was enjoying himself. His tie was now off and the vest to his Black Cashmere suit was open. On his feet he wore a pair of Gucci shoes with the two G's in 14K gold, that had a few drinks spilled on them. He walked up to Rockie and told her if she wanted to talk, they should find a place that was not as noisy. She agreed. They walked out of the ballroom and into a small office down the hall. The office was decked out with a flat screen T.V with surround sound and a big desk that had a built-in coffee maker on top. "So, Raquel, what can I do for you?" Ty asked. "Well first, I wanted to thank you personally for them stacks you gave to my sister and me. I also wanted to say congratulations, I was told you got drafted to the NBA. I know my father is looking down on you with a big smile, he always talked about you. That is what brings me to this conversation. Ty, I don't believe the person that murdered my father is dead. Uncle Fresh is way too calm about...." Ty stopped her. "This is a very serious issue for you I see. But let me tell you this, the dudes that were involved in your father's death, do not exist anymore. You have my word on this." Ty explained. "No offense Ty, but my gut is telling me he's still out there. I won't rest until I know for sure that he's dead!" Rockie said with anger. "Girl If you don't sound like your father, with that attitude and that look in your eyes." Ty smiled at her. "Ok Raquel, where do you think we should start looking for his killer? Better yet, do you even know where to start?" With a smile on her face she said. "I'm glad you asked. Now I know for a fact, that Fresh ain't doing the things he used to while my father was alive. I figured If I am doing my one-two thing, it could make things better for you and me. Then and only then, will we get closer to my father's killer. Once the numbers go up, the killer will be losing money. I know that's the reason my father was murdered in the first place." Rockie finished talking then took a gulp of her drink. "Raquel, you are definitely your father's child. I will tell you what, because I love the idea, I will have a talk with my partner and get back to you. Give me your cell phone number and I will call you in a few days. Bet?"

"Sounds like a plan. Hopefully, you will agree with all of this. I would hate to have to go elsewhere. I will not rest until this job is done." She gave her number to Ty after she finished her drink. "Ok girl let us get back to this party. We don't want to miss this performance." They headed back to the party where the sounds of Jay-Z feat. Kanye and Rihanna's "Run This Town" bounced off the walls. The crowd sang along while dancing and acting crazy. Games and his team were now a little drunk and on the dance floor, doing what it do. Rah Rah was now up and dancing after she finished her Margarita. She had a glass of Rosé before that, so she was tipsy. Rah Rah was not a drinker and felt the effects of the alcohol kicking in. She danced closely to Games and planned on keeping him in her sights tonight. Ty and Hots, along with Ty's wife and sister, stood on the stage they had set up. Ty looked at his watch and saw they had less than 5 minutes until the ball dropped. He pressed a button on a remote that made two 70-inch flat screens appear from the ceiling. Ty grabbed a microphone and turned it on. "For those of you who love to watch the ball drop, like myself, I made sure that you didn't have to miss it. Yall could be anywhere else, but yall are here with me and mines. So let's continue to ball!" The crowd went wild. Ty told the servers to make sure everyone had a bottle of their own before the ball dropped. By now Fresh, Games and their team were close to Latasha and the girls, as they stood on their feet with bottle and drinks in the air. Ty told the DJ to turn the music off. Everyone's attention was now on the TV's. There was less than a minute to go and everyone counted down starting at 10. "10, 9, 8, 7, 6, 5, 4, 3, 2, 1." The crowd yelled. "Happy New Year!!!" Suddenly, the lights went out. You could here all types of commotion until the lights came back on. Alicia Keys appeared on stage singing the "New York" hook. The crowd was beyond hyped at this point. Once the beat dropped, Jay-Z made his grand entrance on stage and rocked the place. All that were in attendance began to sing and rap along.

# CHAPTER 14

G-money pulled up in front of Trump Plaza. He had just gotten off the phone with Rockie and told her he would be there in 15 minutes. G-money stood by the passenger side of his car, waiting for Rockie and her peoples. He noticed VVS and Rockie walking in his direction. "Hey G-babe." Rockie said in a sexy but drunk tone. "Look at my future, one too many, huh?" " No, not really, I could use one more shot. Think you could assist me?" "Ma, I am your assistance. No need for the silly questions, now let us get you out of this cold. And how are you doing tonight VVS?" G-money asked while opening the car door to let Rockie in. "I'm good, you just take care of my sister and have her home first thing in the morning." VVS said. G-money gave her a head nod before jumping in his car and throwing it in drive. He turned up his favorite song by Plies and T-Pain. "Shorty". All Rockie could do was smile. She knew she was the reason he loved this song so much.

---

ROCKIE COMPLIMENTED G-money on his home when they arrived and pulled into the parking garage. From the outside you could tell it had a warm motherly touch to it. "Thanks. This is my mother's house, even though I help pay for it. Now come on, I want you to meet her and my little sister." Rockie looked shocked when he mentioned his sister.

G-money never told Rockie he had a sibling. G-money opened her door, took her coat, and grabbed Rockies hand. They walked through two doors that led them to the upstairs part of the house. Instead of heading straight upstairs, G-money opened a door that led into the kitchen. The kitchen was decked out with Red Wood cabinets and had tiles on the floor of the same color. Rockie could tell they spent a nice piece of change on the interior decorating.

The living room was no different from what Rockie had seen so far. There was a plush, white carpet under a dark Grey leather sectional couch. The couch was so big, it went around damn near the entire living room. There was a

62-inch flat screen that sat on the wall in the corner that was covered with mirrors and flowers. "This is really nice G-money." "You still looking for that other shot? Because you sure don't need it calling me G-money." "Yeah. You know I am still a little twisted. I didn't even hear myself say that. Anyway, where's your mother and little sister?" "They must've fell out waiting on us. We watched the ball drop and ate some of mommy's cooking while listening to some oldies but goodies. You know I had to press my mother to try some Rosé and she loved it. While she was not looking, I snuck Diamond a small glass too." "You're always doing something you ain't got no business doing." "Well, that's why their asses is knocked out now. We might as well go upstairs and enjoy this bottle of Rosé." He said with a smile. They made their way up to G-moneys bedroom, that was also decked out. Rockie was impressed by the décor. He had plush Black wall to wall carpet, a Queen-sized bed, a Red leather Lazy boy and a 52-inch flat screen. G-money had a surround sound system with a CD/DVD rack. With a push of a button, the remote control he had, controlled just about everything in his room. Nicki Minaj's "Your Love" came pouring through the speakers of his radio. "This my shit right here, what you know about this?" Rockie asked while getting her two-step on. G-money just laughed as he sat the remote on the bed. He poured them each a drink and passed Rockie her glass. "Raquel, you've made me the happiest man alive for the New Year. And I promise to never, ever hurt you.... You hear me girl?" G-money used his empty hand to lift her chin up to face him. "Yes Glen, I hear you. All I want is for you not to hurt me." Rockie explained. He bent his head down and kissed her passionately. What felt like an eternity was only under a minute. "Hold up a second ma, I got something for you." G-money headed over to his walk-in closet. Not a second later, he came out holding a sheer lavender night by David Yurman. "That's pretty, especially the color." She said while reaching for it "You know I wouldn't forget my future's favorite color." "Thank you, baby. But where am I going with this?" "I thought you might've wanted to be comfortable and sexy at the same time. But you can always sleep in it or...." He paused as he as he stepped back in the closet "....my favorite football jersey and still look just as sexy." He threw his Pittsburgh Steelers jersey at her. Rockie frowned her face up. "Nah, I'll pass. I wouldn't want you thinking you could tackle me once I put this on." "It really don't matter what you have on, you can get tackled either way." "Whatever! Now show me to the bathroom, so I can get cleaned up and change." G-money walked her to the bathroom. He let her do her thing after giving her two wash clothes and a towel. G-money turned the shower on and showed Rockie how to adjust the temperature of the water. G-money propped himself up on his two pillows in a wife beater and a pair of cotton pajama pants made by Polo. He was watching "Meet The Browns" the Tyler Perry Movie. G-money was laughing at Mr. Brown, with his ashy knees and tight basketball shorts, when Rockie walked in. G-moneys eyes damn near popped out of its sockets. "Damn girl, you are definitely a goddess, my future." Rockie walked over to the bed, still somewhat embarrassed. He sensed it and began to comfort her. "Get over here before I jump on and tackle you." That put a smile on her face as she climbed in bed. She was so nervous she reached for her glass on the nightstand and took a big gulp. G-money was still admiring her 34C-25-43 frame as he grew a hard on. He grabbed his personal bottle of Henny and took a swig. "You had to pull out something stronger, huh?" Rockie asked. "Yeah, pretty much. After seeing you, I needed a shot of something that burns the chest. "Well let me get a shot too." She pushed her glass in his face. He poured her a swig, and she took a deep breath before taking it back. G-money took her glass from her and sat it on the nightstand. He laid next to Rockie and began kissing her. Rockie's nipples got hard almost as fast as G-money kissed her. Her nipples poked out of the sheer nighty, poking G-money in his chest as he began to rub on them. He made his way down to her nipples and began sucking on then through the nighty. "Babe, take it easy, kay?" Rockie said between moans. G-money lifted his head up and said, "I promised you I wouldn't hurt you." He sucked on a nipple. "You could take that to the bank." He went back to what he was doing. G-money kept in mind that Rockie was a virgin. You would never expect it with the way she acted. But he had all intentions of pleasing her to the fullest. G-money made his way down to her thong. He slid them off and gently started sucking and licking on her pussy lips and clit. "Oh...my god. Babe it feels...sooo good." Rockie moaned. He stayed down there until he made Rockie cum back to back. G-money took his pajama pants off and grabbed a Magnum out of his nightstand. Rockie sat up to help G-money put the condom on. "Are you sure you can do this?" G-money asked. "Babe, I know I told you I was a virgin, but this shouldn't be that hard." Rockie opened the condom and began to put it on. She could not believe how big G-money was down there. After putting the condom on, she laid on her back and spread her legs wide. "Babe be easy. You're not no little nigga." G-money couldn't help but smile at her comment as he climbed on top of her. "If this shit hurt, he's gonna have to stop." She thought to herself. G-money used the tip of his dick, until he got her wet and hot. After slowly guiding himself inside, he started sucking on her nipples and made his way up to her lips. Rockie bit down on his lip and dug her nails in his back. That didn't stop G-money and before she knew it, Rockie was trembling from another orgasm. Rockie had loosened up and was now moaning and screaming how she wanted all of G-money. He threw both of her legs over his shoulders and went in. "Oh yes!" G-money was putting in work for a few minutes before Rockie asked to be fucked doggy style. Without hesitation, G-money did just that. They went at it like animals for the next few hours. The sun started to rise as they fell asleep.

# CHAPTER 15

Fresh parked his black '08 Cadillac Escalade in front of a tall beige and brown building on Carlton Ave. He was in Brooklyn picking up his date for the night. Fresh became a loner after Swift's death, but he did not hang up his players jersey. The only dudes you would catch him hanging with was Games and his team. After what happened to Swift, Fresh didn't trust Niggas. He made an exception for Michelle today. Fresh met her at the New Years party a few weeks ago. As stunning as she was, it was the conversation and what she did for a living that caught his attention. Michelle was in her $5^{th}$ year as teller at Citi Bank and she was an industry party promoter outside of banking hours. Fresh liked her style, She was 38 years old with a 5-year-old son. Her son's father was up north serving a 15 year to life sentence for murder. It was their second date since New Year's and Fresh had every intention on scoring tonight. After parking his truck, he walked into her building and pressed her intercom. "Who is it?" said a female voice asked. "Uh, its Fresh, Is Michelle in?" The door made a buzzing sound then opened. "She said come up, she's not quite ready yet." The same voice said. Fresh walked to the elevators and made his way upstairs. When he got to the door, a younger version of

Michelle but with longer hair opened the door. "Hey, how you doing...Fresh you said, right?" "Yeah. That is me. How are you?" Fresh replied and asked. "I'm fine, come in and have a seat. I'm Toya, Michelle's little sister/babysitter. She'll be with you in a second." Fresh admired Michelle's apartment. He could tell she had expensive, but beautiful taste. Toya came back in the living room to offer him something to drink but he declined. A few minutes passed before Michelle came from the back room. Michelle looked gorgeous. She was rocking the hell out of her long sleeved Dolce & Gabbana, full body dress and a pair of Jimmy Choo knee high boots with a 5-inch heel. Fresh complimented her on how beautiful she looked, and they were on their way. Before walking out the door, Michelle screamed to Toya that she did not want any of her hoodlum friends in the house. The minute they were gone Toya called her boyfriend to see if he could come see her.

---

TWO-FACE SAT on his couch smoking a blunt while watching the Biggie Smalls movie "Notorious" for the fifth time. His baby mother was in the bedroom on her Desperate Housewives shit, so he went to the living room. "I knew I should of went to the strip club tonight." Two-Face said to himself as he watched the scene when Lil' Kim was fucking Biggie. He rubbed his dick before saying "I need some pussy tonight" out loud. Just as he finished his thought, his cell phone vibrated. When he looked at his phone, he could not believe his luck. He picked up and turned the T.V. up. "Yo." "Face, what up boo." "Ain't shit, what's good with you?

"Nothing much. I'm babysitting for my sister, she just left to go to dinner. And I was wondering if you wanted to come through." "Sounds like a plan, so your sister dating again, huh? Now she know Big Kev would not be jacking that if he was home. What bozo she fucking with now anyway?" "I don't know, some nigga named

Fresh. But who cares, are you coming over or what? We don't have all night." "You said Fresh?" Two-Face asked, getting up off the couch. "No, I said Fresh, why?" "Don't be a smart ass. Aight then, I should be there in like 20 minutes." He hung up and could not believe his luck. Two-Face wanted to call Nitty, but he figured he should get all the details first. Two-Face knew he had to fuck fire out of Toya quick. He grabbed a jar of sour, two blue dolphin pills and the rest of his Hennessey.

Two-Face told his baby mother he had something important to care of before walking out the door.

———————

GAMES, Ratley and D-nice sat in Game's truck, smoking a blunt while listening to a Lil' Wayne mix tape. They sat in front of Ocean Ville, where Games was from. He had O.V. on smash right now. With the help of Fresh, he planned to take over Far Rock the same way. For right now, he had to keep his goons together. "Yo D-nice, you got to stay in O.V. until I make sure everything is good money. It has been about two months now and that nigga Black still in a coma. And if he don't make it, I'm pretty sure these niggas ain't going to do no talking." "Games, I understand all that, but if I move out there, who's going to help Drake out here? Besides, Its gonna look like I'm scared or something." "Check it D-nice, put your pride in ya back pocket and sit on it. I did not get to where I am at dealing with my pride. The first time I met Fresh, may god bless the big homies soul, he told me 'If you're going to be on my team, leave your ego at home.' You know he asked me to go to the store for him for $10, come on $10? But it was a test, which I came to learn later." Games got so caught up in his story, he reminisced back to the days when Swift was alive. "Yo games." Ratley shouted for the third time. "You act like you don't want to smoke." Ratley continued while tying to pass the blunt. Games snapped out of his thoughts then took the blunt. After a long deep pull he said "Yo

Nice, don't worry. Your pay remains the same, you'll just be in a different location, ya dig?" "Aight man, whatever." D-Nice. said. "Matter of fact, let me hit Fresh up really quick." Games said as he pulled his phone out and began to dial. Fresh picked up on the third ring. "What's the business lil' bro?" "Ain't too much of nothing big bro. I was just hitting you up to see what your boy Nitty had to say." Games replied. "Oh yeah, that's taken care of as of right now, but you know how to remain. Sleep is the cousin of death, ya dig? I never really liked that dude anyhow, but the big homie fucked with him." "Yeah, I can dig it." "Anyhow, I am out with a beautiful young lady right now, so you already know. I'll give you a ring in the A.M." "Ok bro, you already know in the A.M." they both hung up. "So everything good?" Ratley asked. "Yeah, for right now. But even when I'm sleep, the hammers are up, ya dig?" "Yeah, whatever my nigga."

D-Nice said. "Where in hell are these bitches at? It's been about a half an hour already." Ratley asked. "You know these joints coming from the Bronx, so give them a minute. And you better hope its three of them or you're out of luck." Games said while laughing. " You better call them bitches and find out, because I'll be gone right now." Ratley said with an attitude. "Yo, hold up a minute. How the fuck D-Nice get first dibs?" as Games was about to speak, D-Nice interrupted him. "You don't have to explain nothing to this nigga. It ain't our fault this nigga don't leave Queens." "Nigga, you only made it to the Bronx because the nigga Gucci took yall out there." Ratley said. The fellas smoked another blunt and went back and forth until Crystal called. Her and the girls called for directions from the airport. Games asked himself "How the fuck them dingy Bronx bitches get to the airport? Oh well. Fuck 'em!"

# CHAPTER 16

Clarence, Dre, and Cuban were creeping through the back of Red Fern. They wore all black and carried 16-shot Glocks. They were headed to building 12-70. Drake and Lance had been bussing sales there for the past 2 hours. Cuban went through the back, so that no one could escape. He really hoped nobody ran through the back, he didn't want to shoot anyone today. Drake noticed the dark figure come out from around the building. "Oh shit, it's a hit." He screamed towards Lance. Lance backed out the 357 Magnum and let Drake get past him before squeezing two shots in the figure's direction. The shots were already coming in their direction when Lance was hit with a bullet in his leg. He squeezed two shots in the door as he fell to the floor. One of the two hit Clarence in the chest, sending him flying back and dying before he hit the ground. Dre ducked down and opened the door from the bottom. Once opened, he squeezed a few shots in the building. Lance dropped one of the figures, not knowing it was two of them. When he stood up to run for the stairs, he was hit once in the leg and twice in his back. Lance fell to the floor on his face. Dre ran inside and put two more shots in the back of his head. Dre kept running towards the back door where Cuban was. Cuban was ready to squeeze the trigger until he noticed it was Dre running through. "Yo, what the fuck happened in there?" Cuban asked. "No need for questions right now, Drake got away and Clarence got hit. Let us stick to the plan and get the fuck out of here." They both took off running through the back streets, hopping into a parked car that was waiting for them.

---

"OOH BABY, THAT FEELS GOOD." Rockie said to G-money as he gave her a foot massage. "It feels so good because you walk around in heels all day. I know your feet be killing you." "Oh shut up and handle your business." Rockie said laughing.

G-money jumped on her and they began wrestling on his bed. Since their episode on New Year's, they have been inseparable. They could not seem to get enough of each other. Everyday G-money would pick her up from school, she would stay at his house until it was time for her to go. Today was one of those days. "Ok,ok,ok." Rockie said as G-money tickled her. "Glen, stop it before I pee on myself." "Don't worry, I'll clean you up." He said as he began to kiss her neck. "Don't you start, you know Zoe will be here in a few minutes." G-money was starting to feel some type of way and tried his best not to say anything. Rockie was beginning to learn his ways well and sensed it. "Do I sense a little jealousy?" She asked. G-Money had to play it cool. "Ma, why would I be jealous over some dirty ass African?" "Glen, you don't do a very good job hiding your jealousy, or whatever it is you are feeling." "To be honest, its not so much about Zoe. It is the fact that I feel like you are hiding another life. Ma, I want the chance to be your every-thing. That means if you must get home, I will get you there. Shit, even If I have to buy you a car myself." "I understand what you're...." Rockies phone rang interrupting her mid-sentence. It was Zoe calling to let her know he was outside. "Give me a minute Zoe, kay?" Zoe agreed and hung up. Rockie turned her attention back to

G-money. "Listen babe, we agreed that you will meet my family on my birthday. You will also learn where I live. You won't have to feel this way anymore soon enough." Rockie got up to put on her ACG boots while getting herself together to leave. G-money put on a robe to walk her outside. On their way out, Rockie said goodnight to G-moneys mother and sister. She gave them both hugs and kisses on her way out. "I'll see yall tomorrow." She said over her shoulder while walking out the door. G-money held Rockie in his arms as they leaned against Zoes parked Range Rover. "Raquel, I've never told any of my girlfriends this, but I love you. And you are special to me, along with those two other women in there. Please do not be offended by how I act sometimes, ok?" "No more to be said. Just remember what LOVE stands for." "How could I forget? Loyalty Over Values Everything." " Well.... LOVE." Rockie said then kissed him passionately. "Ok you two, yall had all day for that." Zoe said interrupting their kiss. G-money opened the passenger side door and helped Rockie get in. Once she was in, he told her to call him when she got home. "Zoe, make sure my future gets home safely." Zoe put his thumb up. Zoe pulled off and headed to the highway. When he pulled up to a red light, he reached behind him and took out a wad of money. "Here you go Boss lady." He tossed her the cash. "Don't worry its all there, but you can still count it." "Now you know you don't have to tell me that Zoe. I don't trust my right hand when I'm counting my own money." They both laughed while Rockie began counting. Rockie had been giving Zoe money to flip for her for the past three weeks. She knew he liked to push that sour diesel, so she offered to buy a few QP's. (Quarter Pounds)

Today he gave her 4 stacks off one of the 3 QP's she brought. Paying only $2,400 a QP and making $1,600 was not too bad of a profit. Especially when Zoe flipped a QP every day. "All here." She said after counting it up. "You knew it would be, stop playing." Zoe responded. "So what you need Zoe?" "I don't need anything but some sleep. I have been out since 9 this morning. And I only got about 4 to 5 hours of sleep last night." "Well, well, who's the lucky girl?" Zoe frowned up his face. "Nah, its not that type of party. Her name is sour patch." They both started laughing. They pulled up to Rockies house. Before getting out, Rockie asked Zoe about some other business they had spoke on. "Oh, I got some people that would fuck with me if I had some good shit, I'm sure of that. Boss lady, you're really trying to push some of that shit, huh?" "You'll see soon enough Zoe, just give me a few. I'm lining it all up as we speak." "Well you know I'm here for you. Have you ladies thought about what yall gonna do for the B-day?" Zoe asked. "We're off to M.I.A. My mother and uncle are paying for us and VVS to stay for three days." "Sounds like yall going to have a ball out there." "We sure will! Let me get in this house. I'll see you tomorrow Zoe." They said their goodbyes before Rockie walked in the house. As soon as she walked in, Soulja came running to the door. Soulja was a champion line, Shih-Tzu dog the girls bought their mother for Christmas. "Hey Soulja, how you doing boy?" Rockie asked while picking him up and walking into the living room. She rubbed on his fur and played with him while asking Racheal what she was doing in the living room. The living room was almost never occupied. "I felt like watching a movie in here. And I was also waiting on you." Rah Rah said. This was one of the reasons why Rockie felt like the oldest and in charge of things. Rah Rah still acted like a baby when it came to the two. She felt like she could not go to bed without Rockie, sometimes she could not even eat without her. "So what's up twin?" Rockie asked " Well, I've been on the phone for about an hour and..." Rockie interrupted her. "Spit it out!" "I like Games." Rah Rah said. "Oh shit...." "You better stop cursing before mommy hear you." "Its about time you like somebody. But why Games of all people? Games has been like the cousin/brother we never had."

"I don't know honestly. He's so sweet and funny." "And don't forget black as hell" Rockie added. They both started laughing. Rah Rah cut the T.V. off and took their conversation upstairs to Rockies room. Rockie wanted Rah Rah to finish telling her story while she got herself prepared for bed and ready for school the next day.

# CHAPTER
## 17

Fresh was laying in his bed when he got the phone call about the shoot-out that took place in Red Fern last night. Today he was supposed to get up with Nitty so they could talk. Not the one to like coats, Fresh threw on his Black and Brown HoBo leather over his Brown Champion hoody. Under all that, he had on his Teflon vest. Because Fresh was already a large man, weighing a little over 230 pounds and standing at 6'2", the vest made him look bigger. His Roc and Republic jeans along with his brown ACG boots completed his look as he stepped out of his Long Island home. It was a two-family house that he shared with his parents. He decided to take the Jag because the snow was melting into slush. When in the car, he called Nifty's phone. The phone rung several times before the answering machine picked up. He left a quick message saying he was 15 minutes away from their meeting location. Fresh then threw his car in drive and headed to JFK airport. The loud music that was playing from Nitty's Benz was the reason he did not hear his phone ring. He sat parked waiting on that phone call but got caught in the zone smoking a blunt with Two-Face. "So what time are you meeting up with this dude?" Two-Face asked. Nitty snapped out of the trance he was in. "He should've called me by now." Nitty looked at his phone and noticed he missed a call. He called the number back and told Two-Face to turn down the music as he waited for Fresh to pick up. "What up Nitty?" "What it do? My bad, I didn't hear the phone." "Its all good. Check it though, I'm at the port in 5 minutes. Usual spot, ya dig?" "Aight, I'm on my way." Nitty hung up and told Two-Face he would call him when he gets back. They gave each other dap before Two-Face exited the car. Nitty could not wait to get Fresh out the way. With the information Two-Face dropped in his lap it was only a matter of time. Nitty found out that Fresh was seeing his homeboy Big Kev's baby mother, Michelle. He also had the drop on Fresh because Two-Face was fucking Michelle's sister. "Fresh will be too caught up in the pussy and get caught slipping." Nitty said to himself out loud. Nitty thought about executing his plan the whole 20-minute ride to the airport. When he pulled into the parking lot, he drove around until he found Fresh laid back in his Jag. Nitty parked three cars down, on the opposite side of Fresh. He got out and walked to Fresh's car. When he jumped in the passenger seat, he gave Fresh a dap. "The invisible man?" Nitty asked. "I'm cooling. But check it Nitty, your people are getting besides themselves and I'm not feeling that. Right now you got me looking like I'm not on my job." "Damn Fresh, straight to it huh? As I told you before, the misunderstanding was with two soldiers. One of those soldiers lays in the hospital as we speak, nearly on his death bed. I know I said I would handle it, but you know how these little knuckle head niggas could be." "Aight listen Nitty, I won't ask again. The next time, them little niggas gots to get the fuck up out of Red Fern. I cannot keep supplying you, while yall taking my workers to war at the same time. Not only is it a slap in the face to me, but it is also a slap in the face to Swift as well. You know for a fact if it wasn't for him, the work you push out in Red Fern wouldn't be possible." "Nah, you're right about that, and you got my word. I'll straighten all that out Fresh." "That sounds like the best option. Because anything other than that and we are a wrap, ya dig?" Not letting Nitty answer,

Fresh continued "I popped the trunk, there's two bricks in there. Be careful and holla at me when the time is right." Nitty agreed, gave Fresh a dap, then went to get the work out the trunk so he could be gone.

"AHH PAPI...YES GET IT." VVS moaned while getting fucked from the back by Dro. "Who pussy ma....huh, who's pussy is this?" Dro asked while smacking her ass and watching the waves. They been at it since VVS woke up to Dro and his rock-hard dick. She knew when she got up and saw his dick standing at attention, she would be late for school. "It's yours papi...oh, fuck your pussy papi!" "Oh shit...I'm bout to nut ma. Her it come, Ahhh...fuck!" Dro pulled out and came on her ass. "Every chance you get your going to nut on my ass, nasty." VVS said with a smirk. "You know you like that shit, so stop fronting. Now get your ass up so you can go to school. You know where the bathroom at. VVS got up and put a towel around herself and ran into the bathroom before Dro's cum could roll down her ass cheeks. While VVS was in the shower, her phone was ringing in the bedroom. Dro picked up her phone off the nightstand and saw "Twin 1" on her caller id, so he picked it up. "What's good Rockie?" "Who the hell is this?" Rockie covered her mouth after realizing her mother was standing in the living room, looking right at her. Rockie covered the phone and apologized to her mother. Dro was on the other end of the phone talking, but Rockie never heard him. "Who is this with my sisters' phone?" she asked again. "Hold on Rockie, I'm taking the phone to her now. And what other nigga gonna be answering her phone but Dro!" "Oh, what's good Dro? Good morning. How you doing and all that good stuff?" "Yeah, right back to you and the family, hold on here she go." Dro passed VVS the phone while she was stepping out the shower. She walked in the room to get dressed while Dro hopped in the shower. "So you're getting an early morning fix, huh chicken head?" Rockie said. "Don't hate because you didn't get an early morning tune up on your birthday....Happy Birthday sisters!" VVS yelled through the phone. "Thank you, sister." Rockie said with a big smile on her face. "Oh and you know your other sister is still upstairs doing her hair. Like she going out somewhere, its only school." "Oh please bitch, I know your hair is done for school." VVS said. "Well actually it's not. I have it in a doobie like always. And that is how it is going to stay. Anyways, are you meeting up with us after school or what? I'm trynna get a whip today." "Bitch, you know I'll be there. I wouldn't miss it for the world." "Alright then, let me get off this phone cause mommy dropping us off today. Zoe must've had a long night or something because he would've picked up his phone by now." "Well let me say Happy Birthday to Rah Rah before you hang up." Rockie took the phone to Rah Rah while she went to get her books. After saying Happy Birthday, VVS hung up the phone excited about Rockie buying a car today.


MEANWHILE ON THE other side of Queens, G-money was at Clarence's house in Red Fern. He stopped by to pay his respects to Clarence's mother, his two sisters and little brother. G-Money let her know he was truly sorry for her loss. He reassured her he would not rest until the person involved in this was dead and gone. G-money gave the eldest sister an envelope with 10 stacks in it to go towards anything they needed. He did not give it to the mother because everyone knew she got high. After saying his goodbyes, he headed out the door and outside to the streets. Although it was about 35 degrees outside, G-money wore a blue Yankees fitted with a blue and white Yankees leather made by Mitchell & Ness. He rocked a pair of denim blue LRG jeans with a pair of crisp all white uptowns. He walked to his car that was already running due to his automatic starter. As he jumped in, he thought to give Rockie a call. Realizing that it was close to lunch time, he decided to drive by her school. Before he could pull off, his phone rung, it was Dre. "Yo D, what's good boy?" G-money answered. "Ain't much of nothing G-money. I was just hitting you up to see what was going on with that shorty?" G-money knew all his people needed some work, but he was waiting on Nitty. And that's what Dre was asking for. "Dre, I'm waiting on shorty to call me now. But check it, I am out here now and 50 cents out here crazy. So it's best we give it a few more days anyway. That shit that took place last week done made this shit fish grease, ya dig?" "I can dig it bro. Just know I am on standby when you ready. A nigga fucked up right now, so I'm at the edge." "Aight, I'll give you a call later. You can come pick up a few dollars until shorty come through. And when I call, don't have me waiting. Today is Wifey's B-day so more than likely she'll be with me." "Aight bro, One!" they hung up and G-money began thinking about Nitty and the games he was playing. He decided to call him up and see what the deal was.

# CHAPTER 18

Games and Dro traveled downtown to Canal street to look for a gift for the twins' birthday. They stopped at a jewelry store that caught Games attention. "Damn, that's a nice bracelet, you see that shit Dro?" Games asked. "Yeah, that thing is tough." "Let's go inside and check that out." When inside, a long-haired blonde lady asked if they needed any help. "Yeah Ms. I am looking for something nice for a set of twins that just turned 18. I noticed a pretty tennis bracelet in the window." "That sir is one of a kind. It holds over 2 ½ carats of VVS diamonds, the bracelet itself is platinum." "Ok, well how much would two of those cost me?" Games asked. The lady was surprised at how arrogant Games was, so she had to make sure he understood when she spoke. "Well sir, one of these bracelets alone will run you at least $6,500." She made sure she put emphasis on the price. "Aight, well how long would it take for you to put two of those together? I'ma also need you to customize them. I need the letters "L.O.V.E" engraved on the inside of both. Oh, and don't forget to include the gift wrapping. Now if you could give me a pickup time and how much I will be paying all together, I would highly appreciate it." The lady was standing there in shock. She excused herself to get her manager. 5 minutes later a shorty elderly woman, who appeared to be over 60 years old, came from the back. She said 'Good Afternoon' as she offered her hand to Games. Games shook her hand and noticed the big ass diamond on her wedding ring. The lady explained that she had been informed about what he was asking for and wanted to know how he would be making his purchase. "Cash please." Games replied. The elderly lady gave him a price of $10,500 for everything, if he was going to pay right now. Games had Dro pull the money out a small Louis Vuitton draw string bag. After paying for the bracelets, she told him to come back in an hour and a half to see the engraved bracelets gift wrapped. Games and Dro went to grab something to eat and to see what else they could find in Chinatown.

---

ROCKIE HAD JUST HUNG up the phone with G-money. He was on his way to pick up the twins from school. Rockie and Rah Rah stood in front of their private high school that was heavily populated with white kids. "So....Rah Rah, have you spoken to Games lately?" "Yeah, we spoke last night. He asked what we were doing today. I told him whip shopping and you know he had jokes. Talking about 'Balling'." They both laughed knowing how stupid Games could be. "That reminds me, I have to give Tyrick a call." Rockie said.

"And what are you calling him for?"

"I might need some extra bread for these V's." Rockie had plans on buying her and Rah Rah a car and she wanted to make sure she had enough money. She pulled her phone out and dialed Ty's number. Ty, not familiar with the number, picked up on the second ring.

"Hello?"

"Hello, may I speak to Ty?" Rockie asked.

"Speaking, who's this?"

"This is Raquel, How you doing Ty?'

"Oh shit, how you doing Raquel? Is everything alright? How's the family?" "Everything is cool with the family and me. I called you today because it is me and Rachel's birthday and I need a loan. I'm trying to buy us each a car today."

"Word...today is y'all b-day? That is crazy because my b-day is in two weeks. But that's not what's up yet."

Rockie cut him off "Oh yes it what's up! Aquarius in the building." Rockie said with excitement. "Yeah, well right now, yall are the Aquarius' that is up. Do yall have any idea what type of cars yall want?" Ty asked. "Truthfully. We can't afford nothing too extravagant, so I was thinking something like old BM's."

"Shit, even some old BM's cost. But that shouldn't be a problem." As an after thought Ty asked "Raquel, how much money you got to spend on these cars yall looking for?" "We got a little over 17 stacks." Rah Rah looked at Rockie with a surprised look. She had no idea her sister was holding like that.

"I'll tell you what I'll do for you. I'ma send Hots to you ladies. He'll take yall to a dealer ship and yall can do what it do." "Ty, we really appreciate everything and I'm willing to repay you."

"It's not a problem. As far as you paying me back, you do not have to worry about that. However, I would like to set up a dinner meeting with you some time soon. I'll hit you up with the date before it get here, okay?" "Ok. That's what's up." "Once again, Happy Birthday to you and Racheal. Tell mommy I said hello." Rockie said ok and hung up. No sooner than she hung, G-money pulled up to the front of the school. "You were on the phone for a minute." G-money said in an aggravated tone. "Someone sounds like they have an attitude." Rockie replied. G-money ignored her statement. "Happy Birthday Ladies! I'm not here to argue, I'm here to assist yall with these birthday vehicles and whatever else yall may need." "Well babe, that's what I wanted to tell you. I just got off the phone with my uncle's peoples. They are going to come get us and take us to their own dealership. I hope you are not upset. I'm just finding out about this now." You could see the disappointment on his face, but like always, he tried hiding it. "So now what?" he asked. "We are going to my house. Todays the day you get to meet my mother. We are going to chill until my uncle's peoples come. I promise babe, soon as we get back, we will get up. I shouldn't take long." G-money just kept driving and didn't say too much. Rockie gave him directions to their home in Bays Water.

## CHAPTER 19

Nitty and Two-Face were in Red Fern at Nitty's shorty's house. They just finished kicking it with G-money. G-money broke out to handle his business. Now it was just Nitty and Two-Face sitting in the living room talking. "Yo Face, you think this nigga G-money getting too big for himself?" Nitty asked. Two-Face really wanted to say, "Nigga you getting to big for yourself." But instead he said "Nah, he just see the bigger picture like you. You just not letting him do what he do, you know the boy is a young gunner." Two-Face explained. "But did you see how he was talking? Like he the only nigga that bust his gun." G-money had to let Nitty know he should not have to be put on hold or be told when and when not to fire. In G-money's words, "These niggas don't deserve to be holding this shit down out here. I'm the one pulling these niggas skirts, remember?" he asked Nitty. "Yeah, the lil' nigga is definitely feeling himself." Nitty said

"He don't have to wait too long. Toya told me this nigga Fresh suppose to be taking Michelle out Saturday night. We need to start putting this shit together now." Two-Face explained. "Well shit, pass the blunt and let me hear what you have in mind."

Two-Face passed the blunt and went into detail about how they were going to catch Fresh slipping. As Nitty smoked and listened, he pictured it going down. It sounded like the perfect plan so far. "Alright. Now that all sounds good, but how do we know he'll be bringing her home and not put her in a cab?" Nitty asked. "Because Toya told me he always brings her home. We just got to hope he follows his same routine."

---

LATASHA WAS the first to hear the Horn beeping as the Maybach pulled up. She walked over to the door and pulled the curtain back. "Raquel and Racheal, your ride is here." She yelled out to them. They came running down the stairs as if they were racing to the car. "I know yall ain't running up in this house." Latasha said. "Mommy, uncle Fresh is on the phone." Rah Rah said while passing the house phone to her. VVS sat in the kitchen having something to drink and watching the cake Latasha was baking. G-money came downstairs after the girls. He walked into the living room and gave Latasha a hug and a kiss on the back of her hand. G-money made sure to tell Latasha that he appreciated her comfortability with her daughter. "Ok Glen. You take care and be safe. Always remember that change and growth is something you have to welcome if you plan on being anything in this cold world." "Thank you, Mrs. Williams, once again, it was nice to meet you." They all went outside to leave Latasha and Soulja alone to tend to the cake that was in the oven. Rockie walked with G-money to his car, "Babe what are you about to get in to?" "Nothing much. I guess I could go buy my future something else for her birthday, since I won't be spending no money on a car for her." "I won't be long babe, so try not to get lost in buying my present, kay?" "My phone is right here, waiting for you to call it. Now go on, so you could get back." G-money hugged her tight and gave her a passionate kiss. Rockie walked toward the Maybach and thought to herself. "Damn, that boy loves me." She felt the same way but did not know if it was the right feeling to have. Inside the Maybach, Ty's right hand man Hots, sat in the back as the girls got in. "Hello ladies." Hots greeted them. They twins said hello at the same time. Hots told the driver where to go and they were off. Rockie tossed Hots the bag of money while the car was in motion. Hots caught the bag and then tossed it to the floor like it was nothing.

"First and foremost ladies, Happy Birthday." He waited for them to say thank you and continued. "It's nice to see yall again. That goes for you was well VVS. Do you ladies know what type of vehicles yall looking for? I am just letting you ladies know, there are a lot of cars to choose from. You don't have to have a specific type." Hots said with a smile. He passed each ladies an empty glass from the mini bar. Opening a bottle of Nuvo he said, "It might be too early, but it's a special day so why not?" They rode for the next 20 minutes drinking and talking shit. Hots was crazy cool and had them laughing the entire ride.

They pulled up in the Gun Hill section of The Bronx. The chauffeur parked the Maybach on the curb where the car dealer sat. The chauffeur made his way around to the door and let everyone out. Rah Rah not being a drinker, was already tipsy and almost fell while getting out of the car. "Girl, go ahead and fall on your face if you want." Rockie said as they all laughed. They walked on to the car lot and began looking around. The girls could not believe how many different cars and trucks they were able to choose from. "Rah Rah, whatever you get, you won't be able to drive home. You are too damn saucy off that bullshit." VVS said. "That was an accident stupid. Ain't nobody drunk, so be quiet and help me look for a car." Rah Rah fired back. Racheal and Raquel, I was told to let yall get whatever yall want. Once again, Happy Birthday and have fun trying to choose." Hots said with his arms out, welcoming the girls. After about an hour and a half after modeling inside different vehicles, Rockie and Rah Rah were finally doing their paperwork. They were more than happy about the cars they chose. After looking over 15 cars Rah Rah fell in love with the 2010 BMW X6. It was all white, sitting on 22-inch Forgiato designer rims with an all-black leather interior. Rah Rah was happy as hell and could not believe this car was going home with her. Rockie, being the boss she felt she was, decided she would take the 2010 Range Rover Sport. It was candy apple red and sat on 24-inch Hipnotic wheels. They were a matte black color with red rivet insert rims. The interior was a peanut butter color with red piping.

"I can't believe we're leaving with these cars. Thank you so much Ty." Rockie was saying through her phone. She had to call Ty and thank him again. They never imagined they would be buying these types of vehicles off the lot. "Well, you know y'all deserve the best. And from what I hear, you ladies chose just that, the best."

"If it wasn't for you, none of this would be possible."

"Now I can't take all the credit. Mr. Williams is 75 percent the cause of this. Just make sure you play your cards right as if you were Swift himself, ya dig? Before I let you go, enjoy your birthday weekend in Miami. We will get up when you get back." Rockie thanked Ty once again and hung up. The paperwork was done, and the ladies were now ready to leave. Before getting in their cars, Hots stopped them. "I was going to use this money for a nice time piece or something but ya might need it more to shop 'till ya drop out there in M.I.A." Hots threw the bag of money to Rockie. "Happy Birthday Twins!"

Rockie caught the bag and them jumped in her truck, she called Rah Rah and put her on speaker. "Follow me if you chicken heads want to get home, you know I got the GPS." They all laughed. Rah Rah was not that drunk anymore. Once she saw what type of cars, they were able to pick out, her ass sobered right on up. VVS rode shot gun with Rah Rah even though she promised she was fine. Rah Rah had every intention of driving her car off the lot, no one else.

# CHAPTER 20

"I still can't believe my girl is in a better V than me. What type of shit is that? I got to go buy the Roll Royce Ghost tomorrow." G-money said jokingly after admiring Rockies Range Rover. They were in front of Rockies house, where G-money met back up with them. "Its alright to have your girl riding like the big boys do. Shit, my mother had the Range, so don't trip." Rockie was feeling herself. VVS and Rah Rah came out the house looking fabulous and ready to go. G-money was taking all three ladies out to dinner. He even extended the invitation to Latasha, but she politely declined. She did think it was sweet of him to offer though. "We are ready to eat Rah Rah said stepping into her car. Before she could get all the way in, her mother came to the door. Racheal, did you call that boy Reggie back? He's been calling since you left earlier." "No mommy, I haven't. I'll call him right now." Rah Rah pulled out her phone to make the call. Rockie walked to the passenger side of the Range and threw the keys at G-money. "Here you of babe, it is my birthday, right?" "So you want...yeah I get it. Anything for you my future. I couldn't wait to push this pretty shit anyway." G-money said with a smile. With Rah Rah leading the way, they pulled up to the 59th street side in the back of Ocean Village, where Games was from. When Rah Rah called him earlier, he told her to stop by before they go out to eat. Games had presents for her and Rockie. Of course when G-money seen where Rah Rah was leading them, he became suspicious. He then realized he left his gun in the stash spot of his car. "Ma, what are we doing out in O.V.?" he asked. "We came to see some people really quick, why what's up? You got this look on your face like you're in danger." Nah, ain't nothing. You know how the projects be, dudes don't like other dudes and shit." "Listen babe, we won't be here for long, plus no one can even see you inside this truck." When they double parked behind each other, Rah Rah noticed Games and his boys. They were drinking and smoking, listening to some Lil' Weezy playing from Game's truck. Rah Rah got out followed by VVS. Games saw them pulling up and smiled. "Ok! That's how yall do it! Them thangs are looking really crazy." Games said referring to their cars. "Happy Birthday Ri Ri." He said while he gave her a hug with one arm, trying his best not to spill the drink in his hand. "Where's Rockie?" The second he asked that, she was getting out of the Range. He have her a hug as well. "So who's driving you around in that pretty thing?" Games asked Rockie.

"My man, do you mind?"

"Well excuse the hell out of me sister!" They all started laughing.

"Hold on, I got something for ya." Games walked over to his truck to get their gifts. When he came back, he passed the gifts to them.

"Happy Birthday Twins....LOVE!"

The twins looked up at each other surprised. They knew you had to really fuck with their father to know that word. Let alone, how, and when to use and say it. They both opened their jewelry boxes and admired the platinum tennis bracelets. Once the twins saw the letters L.O.V.E. engraved in the bracelets, they wanted to cry. Games downed what was left in his cup and threw it on the floor. He took both twins in his arms. They hugged him tight and in return he did the same. After what felt like forever, they let each other go. "Not out here like this." Rockie said as she wiped a tear from her eye. "You could have waited for this Games." "Thank you, Games. We love it!" Rah Rah said.

"I know them words mean a lot to yall, because your father drilled it in my head. I don't want to hold yall up any longer, so go and have fun. And Ri Ri, promise me you'll call me no matter what time you get in."

"I promise." Rah Rah replied. They all returned to their vehicles. VVS was the last to get back to the car due to her lovey dovey time with Dro. As they pulled off Rah Rah beeped her horn at Games. He threw up his pointer finger while mouthing the words "LOVE". Rah Rah and Rockie both read his lips and repeated it. Games did not know it yet, but he just earned a special place in the twin's heart with that. Anybody who knew the meaning to that word 'LOVE' had to be very close to their father. Rockie could not wait to get back from Miami. She had revenge to seek and an empire to take control over. For now though, she would enjoy her Eighteenth birthday over dinner with her twin, best friend, and boyfriend.

# CHAPTER 21

Standing in front of the store in his Roc-a-Wear bomber jacket, G-money talked to Rockie on the phone. He was on Hassock Street watching his surroundings. As G-money talked through his phone, he watched as the police were bringing two dudes out the back buildings. "Yeah, they locking up two dudes now." G-money told Rockie. "Maybe you should've flew out here to enjoy this nice beach weather with me." Rockie teased. Rockie, Rah Rah and VVS were sitting on the beach in Miami and she had to rub it in his face. Rockie asked G-money to come along but he declined. His exact words were "You should go and enjoy yourself with the ladies for your birthday. I will just be in the way if I go. Besides, I have a few things to handle in this cold weather, snowman shit lil' mama."

G-money smiled when he said it but was now wishing he had gone.

"Maybe I should have. How yall enjoying yourselves though?"

"We are loving it! We not doing much of nothing right now. Just sitting on the beach in this Burberry two-piece. Wishing you were here to rub some suntan lotion on me." Rockie flirted. "Ah man, you're killing me! I'm about to hang up. Let me get off this phone anyway, its way too much police activity out here." Just as

G-money was saying this, Maliah and two of her girlfriends were walking into the store. "Ok babe. You be careful and as soon as you get a chance, call me back." Rockie said. So Maliah could hear him, G-money spoke a little louder. "Ok my future, I'll give you a ring as soon as I'm upstairs."

"Glen, LOVE." Rockie said

"LOVE."

When Maliah walked out the store, she sucked her teeth. "So you mean to tell me I can't get a phone call, but you can stand on the strip and talk to your lil' friend?" she said with an attitude. G-money just looked at her. Dre and the rest of the fellas outside today, looked on confused. When Maliah saw that G-money was not moved by her outburst, she got in his face.

" You trynna act like you don't hear me G-money!"

"Yo Maliah, get out of my face with that corny shit. You act like I'm fucking you or something. By the way, that was my lady, my future, ya dig?" He said all this while pushing her to the side. This pissed her off, Maliah was really obsessed with G-money.

"I'm not good enough for you to talk to in the street, but I'm good enough to suck your dick in your car, huh?" Her statement caught G-money off guard, he had no choice but to keep his cool.

"You know what Maliah, you're right! That is all you are good for, how about you get in my car and I'll let Dre hold the keys this time." He went in his coat to get his keys and threw them to Dre. That pissed Maliah off even more. "Fuck you, you bitch ass nigga. You think you're big shit. Just wait 'till niggas find out the real deal." G-money told Dre he was about to breeze because this bitch was getting on his last nerve. Dre tried to convince Maliah into walking away. Not giving a fuck, she went around him and tried to spit at G-money. G-money heard Maliah making a scene, so he turned around. As soon as he was facing her and Dre, the spit landed right on his coat, just missing his chin. G-money walked up to her pushing Dre out of the way and smacked her so hard, she almost fell to the floor. Maliah's face turned as soon as she stumbled to stay on her feet. She held her face in disbelief as everyone else stared in shock. "Now go get ya father or something bitch!" G-money said as he walked to his car.

---

LATER THAT NIGHT, Fresh was getting himself ready to go out with Michelle. He had been in the bed all day because his stomach had been messing with him. Fresh felt like he had to take a shit, but every time he sat on the toilet, nothing would happen. He took something for his stomach and used the bathroom a few times. Although he was successful at using the bathroom, he still had a funny feeling in his gut. After checking on the girls in Miami, he started getting himself ready for tonight. Before heading out he wanted to see what Latasha was up to, so he dialed her number. "Hello?" Latasha asked. "Hey sis, how you doing?"

"Hey Fresh, what's up with you?"

"Just checking up on you and Soulja."

"We're good. After coming from doing my nails and thangs, Soulja and I went on a walk for about an hour. I am just getting in. I'm about to make me something to eat, Soulja done ate all his food already."

"Ok, sis. It seems like your day is about over. Have you spoken to the girls yet?" He asked

"Yeah. I just hung up with Racheal. Talking about, they're having Piña Coladas at some bar on the beach"

"I told them to have all the fun they can, cause next time I spend money like this on a trip, we all going. Maybe once they graduate, I'm thinking Disney World." Fresh said in an asking tone. "That sounds like we're about to have fun. I have to lose 5 to 10 pounds before I try slipping into a two-piece." They both laughed. "Sis, now you know you still got it. By the way that reminds me, you must meet Michelle and her son. They're beautiful!"

"What?! I know Fresh the Playa-Playa ain't talking like that."

Latasha said with a smile. I'm happy for you. You know its about that time, have a son and start a family of your own. Just do not forget, you'll always have a family over here."

"LOVE." Fresh replied.

"You already know brother, a tear on your face, is a scratch on my heart."

"That's a new one sis. Where you and the big bro be getting this from? I swear bro was good at that."

"That's one we said to one another. Now its time to pass it down to the family." Fresh and Latasha talked for another 15 minutes. Fresh told her he had to go. It was time for him to pick up Michelle for yet another amazing night. He promised to give her a call tomorrow after she came home from Sunday morning service at church. Fresh wanted to plan a dinner date to discuss their family trip further.

---

NITTY AND TWO-FACE were sitting in one of their spots out in Red Hook projects. Two-Face just put fire to a blunt of some Kush. "Yo, I got to call this bitch to find out when I can come through." Two-Face said as he took a deep pull of the blunt. "Yeah, you do that, let me see what's taking this nigga G-money so long." Nitty picked up his phone to call G-money up.

"What's good Nitty?" G-money asked as he rode shot gun in Zoes' truck.

"Where the hell are you? We need to go over some things." Nitty said agitated.

"Yo Nitty, I'm on my way right now. You act like we don't have a few hours. I am in a cab as we speak, I did not feel like driving out here. I should be there in like 15 minutes or so."

"Aight. Let me know when you get in front of the building, I have to come down to let you in." They hung up and Nitty asked Two-Face what was up with shorty. "Everything going as planned."

She said they left out already, so I'm about to slide out over there. Let that nigga G-money know I'll see him tonight."

"If that nigga ever get out here." Nitty said smirking.

"Take it easy with the general, he makes general moves, you can't front. It's whatever though, I'll holla at yall later."

Fresh and Michelle were just pulling in a little after 3 A.M. They had been drinking and dancing the night away.

"I had a great time tonight Fresh, thank you for the company."

"You know I enjoyed tonight just as much as you did. That's why I am hoping we are on for next weekend. I have reservations for a nice room at the Trump Tower hotel. Along with a wonderful weekend planned for the two of us" Fresh said.

"Well, I can't wait. I just need to make sure Lil' Kev's grandmother is still going to watch him." Fresh parked his Jag inside the parking lot, across the street from Michelle's building. On the same side of the street Michelle lived on, Nitty and G-money sat parked in a dusty black Charger. Nitty picked up his phone and called Two-Face.

"Oh." Two-Face said, sounding as if he was asleep.

"Nigga, if you don't get your sleepy ass up, that pussy ain't that good."

"I'm up, I'm up!"

"Aight then, now get the fuck out of there, if you're up. They walking in the building as we speak." Two-Face got up looking for his pants and shit. Toya felt his moving and got up as well. "Yo Toya, they on their way upstairs." She helped him get his stuff together and out the door before Fresh and Michelle came in. Fresh and Michelle shared a passionate kiss before the elevator door opened.

"You don't have to get off the elevator, these things take too long." Michelle said. "I still have to make sure you get in safely baby." Michelle kissed him on the lips before walking to her door and letting herself in. When she was inside, she blew a kiss and told Fresh to call when he got home. Fresh let the elevator doors close and made his way back down to the lobby. He was in a daze when he walked off the elevator and out the building. Fresh was thinking about what Latasha said. How it was time to settle down and start a family. Michelle's been fitting the wifey role he always imagined. Fresh was such in a daze, he never saw the two dark figures walking his way. They had the drop on him, and he did not realize it until he looked up. "What up Fresh?" the hooded figure asked with his gun pointed in Fresh's direction. Fresh went to reach for his gun but it was too late. A bullet hit him in the chest, causing him to fall on his back. Not giving up, Fresh pulled his gun out. There was no time to pull the trigger as G-money kicked the gun out of Fresh's hand.

"Fuck you trynna do with that homeboy?" G-money asked as he bent down to whisper in Fresh's ear "Tell Swift, there's a new Mr. Far Rock that runs this shit." Nitty walked up to Fresh and pointed the Glock 9 at his head. When Fresh opened his eyes and saw Nitty standing over him, he could not believe his eyes.

"I knew you wasn't....to be trusted." Fresh managed to get out as he was spitting up chunks of blood. Those were the last words he got to say before Nitty squeezed two shots in his head. Nitty and G-money rushed to the car where Two-Face was waiting.

# CHAPTER 22

When Fresh's' mother was called to identify the body, her and her husband were praying that this was not happening. After the identifying process was over, Mr. Johnson held his wife as tight as he could. Fresh was their only son and this was a very painful moment. Mrs. Johnson mustered up enough energy to tell her husband they had to call Latasha. It was a little past 4 A.M. and Latasha was in her 3$^{rd}$ dream as the house phone woke her up. She looked at the clock on the nightstand and could only imagine what it was. Her first thoughts was something happened to the twins. Latasha picked up the phone and cleared her throat.

"Hello."

"Hello Latasha, I'm sorry to call you at this time in the morning. Latasha sat up as she heard Mr. Johnsons voice. "Mr. Johnson, What's wrong?"

"It's...It's Jamel. He's...he's dead!"

"No...No, this cant be happening. Where are you guys at right now, Mr. Johnson?

"We're getting ready to leave the coroners office. We are on our way home , since there's nothing we can do now."

"Can yall make it home safely? I can come and pick you guys up if you can't."

"No, its ok baby. We just want you to know what's going on, we know how much Jamel loved you ladies."

"Well Mr. Johnson, I'll be at your house as soon as I get the twins back from Miami, okay?"

"Ok baby. I know the twins will be hurt when they get the news but get them home first at least."

"Ok, Mr. Johnson. Please give Mrs. Johnson my condolences, I'll see you guys shortly."

When Latasha hung up with Mr. Johnson, she immediately called the twins. Latasha told the twins they had to catch a flight back A.S.A.P.! They asked plenty of questions out of curiosity. Latasha explained that it was very important that they get back home, and she would send Zoe to pick them up. She called the airport to book the next flight leaving out of Miami. After playing top dollar with her credit card, Latasha booked the girls a 9:20 A.M. flight headed to NY. Latasha called Zoe and explained the situation. He promised to be at the airport as soon as he was finished his shower and got dressed. Latasha got up and made her a drink at the bar. She sat in the living room and cried until the sun came up.

———————

IT WAS Tuesday and G-money still had not heard from Rockie. He was laying in his bed with his phone right besides him. Knowing they made plans for him to pick her up from the airport had his blood boiling. Getting the phone call from Nitty, saying it was time to pick up his package, made G-money feel a little better. He thought about calling Zoe to see if he heard from Rockie. When he picked up his phone to call, his phone rung. It was Dre.

"Oh Dre, what up?" G-money answered.

"Ain't shit, trynna figure out what the day looking like." Dre said.

"Aight then, get dressed. I will come snatch you up in about an hour. That way, I can run everything down to you."

"Sounds like a date. Should I bring my goon mask, or should I keep it conservative?" They both started laughing.

"Boy you a fool... Nah but keep it D-block." G-money said.

"Aight, just how I like it, in an hour."

G-money hung up and thought "What better day than today to enjoy with my future. I'm about to Far Rock in the Obama and you gone Michelle it." G-money started dialing Zoe's number. Zoe did not answer the first time. He picked up on the 3rd ring when G-money called back.

"What's happening G-money?"

"Ayo, you haven't heard from Rockie since she been back? Cause I've been calling like crazy."

"Yeah with that, something happened in the family. She is going through it right now. Just give her some time, I'm sure she'll come around to calling you." Zoe explained.

"So your telling me you've heard from her to know all of this, right?" Not waiting for an answer, he continued. "With you knowing how I feel, you really not going to tell me what's going on? What type of funny shit is that?" Zoe sensed G-money was upset.

"Listen G-money, its not my place to overstand that. I just happened to pick them up from the airport. As I said before, she's hurting right now. Give her some time. She will call."

"Yeah, what you said Zoe. I'll Holla back. And if you happen to hear from her, tell her I love her and I'm waiting by the phone." G-money hung up. He was frustrated with what he just heard. He did not know what she could be going through that she could not at least call him. G-money thought about if she might have heard about the incident with Maliah. Or worse, something happened to one of the girls. All G-money knew, was he would soon find out.

"First I got to get this package" he said out loud. He washed up and started getting dressed.

---

LATASHA WAS GETTING herself ready before she had to collect Fresh's belongings from the precinct. Mr. and Mrs. Johnson called and asked if she could pick them up. Detective Roberts was the head detective on the case and was scheduled to meet with Latasha. In her Steve Madden boot cut booties, with a 3-inch heel, she walked into her bedroom from the bathroom.

"Ok girls, there's frozen pizza in there until I get back." She said to the twins. They have been laying in Latasha's bed since they came back from Miami. They listened to their mother trying to lighten up the mood with her famous frozen pizza.

"Ma, we're not hungry, if anything, we'll wait until you get back." Rockie said.

"Alright. I will call on my way in to see if yall want anything from out there. Latasha kissed both her girls on the forehead and said "LOVE" before walking out the door.

Rockie sat up against the headboard of her mother's king-sized bed. Rah Rah laid on Rockies lap, while Rockie rubbed her back.

"Don't worry twin, whoever did this won't get away with it." Said Rockie.

"Twin, do you think this same person has something to do with daddy's death?" Rah Rah asked.

"I don't know. But they will die the same twin, I promise you that."

"Raquel, are you going to really get involved with Ty and Hots?"

"Twin, this is the only way I see me getting to daddy's killer. And possibly uncle Fresh's."

"This is very dangerous Raquel, please be careful."

"Don't worry twin, I will. I am going in for one purpose and one purpose only. Whatever extra we get out of the deal, we can use to our advantage." They talked about Rockie's plans for about an hour before Rockie decided to take a shower. She went to turn the water on while Rah Rah got on the phone to see what VVS was doing. During Rah Rah's phone call with VVS, the doorbell rang. When Rah Rah went to answer, she peeked and looked through the curtains. She saw G-money standing there with a bouquet of flowers and a dozen of roses. She opened the door.

"How are you doing Racheal, is your sister in?"

Rah Rah let G-money in and told him to have a seat in the living room. Rah Rah ran up the steps and opened the bathroom door.

"Rockie, guess who's here with flowers and roses?" Rockie stood in the shower and smiled.

"Can you tell him I'll be down in a second?"

Rah Rah did as she was asked to do then continued her phone call.

With her hair still wet, Rockie came down to the living room in her Burberry Robe. You could tell she had Indian in her, based off her complexion along with her flowing black and brownish hair. To G-money, she was the most beautiful girl he had ever seen. "How are you doing my future? I was worried sick, I had to come and check on you. I truly apologize if you feel I've invaded your space." G-money passed the roses to her, she took them and then gave him a tight hug and a long kiss.

"Thank you, G-baby. And I am sorry for not picking up. This is serious." G-money held her with his arms stretched out in front of him.

"Listen ma, you got to believe me when I say I'm here for you in everyway possible."

G-money said while sitting her down on the couch.

"Tell me....is there anything I can do? Talk to me my future."

G-money was not expecting to hear what Rockie was about to say.

"Babe, my uncle was killed the other night. And it is taking its toll on me. I'm trying to keep it together for the sake of my sister and mother."

"Damn baby, I'm sorry to hear that. Do they have any idea who could have done this?"

"Right now we are just waiting. My mother just went to pick up his things from the precinct, so hopefully she will have something when she gets back. I just needed some time to get my thoughts together. I was going to call you."

They went up to Rockie's room. She got dressed putting on a pair of 'House of Dereon' sweats pants and a Baby Phat tank top. G-money and Rockie then made their way to the kitchen. They sat at the table while Rockie ate a bowl of Cookie Crisp while they talked some more. G-money could not stand seeing Rockie like this. Once he learned her uncle passed, he wanted to do everything to help. But how when he might have been the cause of this? He hoped that this was not the same person, because he would not know how to handle it. He stayed at Rockie's house until he had to get up with Dre. They had some business that needed handling. G-money asked Rockie if she would be ok. He also stressed if she needed anything to just give him a call. Rockie walked him to the door and told him to be careful. G-money promised to call her when he got in the house tonight.

# CHAPTER 23

It was a day before Fresh's funeral and Games was sitting in the living room of Latasha's home with Dro. Games and Rah Rah shared the same couch, while Dro say on the wall to wall carpet with VVS. Latasha and Rockie were in the kitchen cooking dinner. Soulja began barking when the doorbell rang. "Racheal get the door, please baby. Thank you." Latasha yelled from the kitchen. Latasha remembered that Fresh was taking his girlfriend out the night he was killed. He wanted them to meet one another because he felt she was the one for him. Latasha was glad Fresh's phone was with his property at the precinct. It allowed her to go through his phone and find Michelle's phone number. When Latasha called Michelle to tell her the news, Michelle had to meet Latasha and give her the rundown.

"Ma it's Michelle." Rah Rah said from the living room. Rah Rah let her in her while Latasha came to the door.

"How are you doing Michelle? Latasha asked.

"I'm fine and yourself?" she asked back. Latasha introduced her to the Twins, VVS, Games and Dro. They went into the kitchen where Latasha offered her a drink. By now, Rockie had made her way to the living room. "It's finally good to meet you. I know you feel the same when I say, I wish it didn't have to be on these terms." Latasha said.

"Yes. I totally agree. I cannot begin to explain how sorry I am about all of this. Fresh was a wonderful man. In the month or so that we were dating, it had been great."

"I know, he always told me about it."

"And vice versa. Fresh always talked about you and the twins, how y'all were the only family he had beside his parents."

"It's been like that way for a long time. Fresh and my husband were the best of friends. They met in grade school and were inseparable."

" Yes. Fresh did mention his brother/best friend Swift. Look, I want to start by saying I am very sorry for all of this. I will give you any information I come across to fix this problem. I mean, I know it will not fix it, but it may help some. As of right now, all I have is...."

Latasha could not believe all that she said but knew there was more to it. They sat talking for over an hour before Michelle had to get home to her son. Being that her sister no longer watched her son, she had to come out of pocket for one. Michelle told Latasha and the twins that she would see them at the funeral, and she would call when she got home safely. They said goodnight to her, and she left as she came. Sad and hurt but feeling a bit better that she told Fresh's peoples what took place.

Latasha sat everyone in the living room and told them to pay attention to what she was about to say. "Listen, everyone in here knows that what's said..." They all cut in and said it with her... "in here, stays in here!"

"Cool. Now with what Michelle told me, her little sister's boyfriend was involved in Fresh's murder. He was supposed to only Rob Fresh and scare him away from being with Michelle. Michelle said the dudes name is Two-Face and he is a friend of her baby's father. He up north somewhere doing 15 to life. This is not the first time they tried keeping a man out of her life. However, it is the first time they took it this far. What puzzles me is, that nothing was taken from Fresh. He had his phone, his money, his watch and even his pinky ring. They even left him with his gun by his side. This is the reason why the detective does not really care. They think this was a beef and Fresh didn't get to his gun in time." Latasha explained.

'So where do we find this Two-Face dude at?" Games asked.

"It will be done. Lets just get ourselves ready to bury Fresh in peace. When this is done, I'll talk to Michelle about getting in touch with Two-Face." Latasha gave them a quick run down on how they should handle things. After she was done, she went into the kitchen and served dinner, never skipping a beat.

---

THE FUNERAL WAS HELD in Long Island where Fresh was born. It was not that big of a funeral due to the Johnsons having a small family. Fresh's parents were in attendance, along with his grandmother and a few distant cousins. Latasha and the twins arrived together. Games and his team came in right before Latasha and the girls came in. Ty and Hots came through to pay their respects and few people from Far Rock came out to do the same. Michelle made it her business to attends Fresh's funeral, even if she did not stay too long. Nitty and two of his crew members showed up right after Michelle left. They literally just missed one another. Although Michelle did not know Nitty like that, she would have remembered him from being with her son's father.

Games and Nitty made eye contact and Nitty gave him a head nod. Games returned it and began walking in Nitty's direction. With his hand out to dap Nitty, he asked.

"Have we met before?"

"Yeah, Once. I to come pick up from Fresh one day and you was there."

"Ok, now I remember, Nitty right?"

"Yeah that's me. I am just here to pay my respects, Fresh was a good dude. He will be missed."

"Yo check it Nitty, how about you take my number and give me a call in a few days. I believe you are aware of the situation in the Fern and I'd like to touch up on a few things."

Nitty took Game's number, with no intention of calling. They dapped each other and Nitty left with his crew.

Ty and Hits were ready to pull off when Ty called Rockie over to the Maybach. His window was done so he talked low. "I'll be calling you tomorrow around noon, so be ready."

"Kay Ty."

Hot's rolled down his window, where Rockie could see him.

"I hope you're ready. In this game, sexy ladies do not last too long, they are too cute."

"Oh, really? Cuz this cutie can be just a dirty if not dirtier." Rockie said while winking at him. She walked away with a switch in her hips. She did not notice she was, until she looked back. Hot's was still staring as he rolled the window up.

"Oh my god! Were we just flirting with each other?" Rockie asked herself. She walked back to her mother, Rah Rah and VVS.

"He is crazy cute though. He lucky I'm in love." Rockie smiled at her most inner thoughts.

"What are you smiling about?" Rah Rah asked Rockie

"Oh, nothing. Just got some good news from Ty, I'll share that with you later though."

"Well did he compliment you on your dress or your hair? That smile was a little too much, I know you twin!"

"Oh please Rah Rah."

Latasha, the twins and VVS rode to the burial site with Mr. and Mrs. Johnson. After dinner Latasha decided to help Mrs. Johnson in the kitchen with the dishes.

"Thank you so much, Latasha, you've been more than helpful."

"No need to thank me momma, your only child was my only

brother. Jamel always acted like the brother I never had, and I loved him."

Mrs. Johnson broke out crying and Latasha went to hold her.

"Don't worry momma, They'll reap what they sow, that's a promise. It will be ok, momma!"

Latasha found herself crying as well while holding Mrs. Johnson tight.

# CHAPTER 24

R ockie pulled her Range Rover up to an empty space on a downtown Manhattan block. There were two different restaurants on the block, so he called Ty's phone.

"What's going on Raquel?" Ty answered.

"Hey Ty. I am outside. I'm not sure which restaurant to go into. There is two on this block."

"It's called Uno's. Its in the middle of the block."

"Ok." Rockie said as she hung up. She grabbed her Gucci purse and headed to the meeting after hitting the alarm on her truck. When she walked into the restaurant, an employee approached her.

"Hello ma'am, by yourself or table for two?" he asked.

"No sir, I'm actually meeting two that's already here."

"Oh excuse me, Ms. Williams, right this way." Rockie was surprised when the man said her name. 'Ty is already famous, and he hasn't even played an NBA game yet.' Rockie thought to herself. The man escorted her to the table where Ty and Hots sat. They both stood to their feet and shook Rockies hand.

"Hello fellas, thanks for having me."

"Nah, you belong here. Let me take your coat." Hots insisted.

He took her coat and placed it on the back of her chair.

"So did you have a hard time getting here?" Ty asked as they sat down.

"Not at all, it was a pretty easy drive."

"You're looking fabulous tonight, you got a date after this?" Ty asked with a smile on his face.

"I was actually taught to dress appropriately when attending a job interview." Rockie winked.

"Well excuse me! You already got the job with an attitude like that." Hots spoke.

"By the way, what would you like to drink?"

"I'll have a Pina Colada, with an extra shot. You know, something light."

"Such a fucking lady." Hots said.

Hots waved the waiter over. Once at the table, hots gave the waiter their drink orders. He then explained that they would be ordering food a little later. When the drinks were served and the waiter gone, Ty began.

"I need you to listen Raquel and listen good because I don't want any misunderstandings. I overstand who your father is and what you might be capable of. However, If I am going to bring you in, you must play by my rules. Do you understand?"

"I'm all ears and heart....so I overstand."

"Aight then. For starters, Hots will be your point of contact. He will make sure everything gets to you safely. I do not want you driving around with anything, maybe a gun if need be." Ty smiled then continued.

" Now I know you may disagree with this, but Hots is going to give you two of his most loyal men..."

Rockie had to cut him off.

"Hold up Ty, I can't have two Bronx dudes come out to Far Rock and help me run it. I have men for that. If necessary, Hots can always meet them. Please Ty, don't make me deal with some dudes I barely even know."

"I'll tell you what. Hots will meet these people of yours and if they don't fit the bill, need I say more?"

"Nope. You have a deal."

They ordered their plates and feasted. While eating, Ty spoke after wiping his mouth with a napkin.

" Welcome aboard Raquel. Your first drop off will be tomorrow morning, so be up extra early. I know momma love goes to church on Sundays. Hots will be calling around 8:30 A.M."

"Ok cool. Do we need to discuss prices and payment or what?" Rockie asked.

"We really don't have to because we are dealing with a young Swift. However, since you asked, just give me twenty off each brick. You will not get a price like that nowhere. With all that being said, are you ready to play with the big boys?"

"I sure am Ty! Now what about these niggas that did this shit to Fresh?"

"I got some people out in Brooklyn whos' investigating. When we find out what the deal is, you'll be the first to know." They finished up their food and Ty asked for the check. On the way at the door Hots held the door, he wanted to get a peek of Rockie's ass.

"Damn, that shit is fat. And it look wild soft." He said to himself.

"Raquel not for nothing, but you look stunning." Hots said admiring her beauty.

"Why thank you, Hots. You're not looking too bad yourself."

Hots and Ty had on jeans, sneakers, and Polo sweaters with no jackets.

"You don't have to say that, I know that I'm in my thug wear right now."

"You still look cute. You look more like a soldier anyway. Like Beyonce said 'I need a soldier'."

"Alright people, can we get in our cars and stop with all that." Ty said as Hots and Rockie laughed. Ty hugged Rockie and said his goodbyes before walking to his 2010 Cranberry Bentley GT and got in. Hot walked her to her truck and opened the door for her.

"Thank you so much, Hots. You're such a gentleman."

"You're very welcome. Anything for someone as beautiful as you."

"Hots are you flirting with me?"

"Well, yes and no. Yes, because you are beautiful. And no because I do not want Swift haunting me. Besides, I know you have a lil' boyfriend."

"How old are you Hots?" Rockie asked.

"I'm 26, why?"

"Cuz you said, my "lil' boyfriend". It makes sense now. By the way, you look good for 26, I would have never guessed."

"Thank you. That is nice to know. I guess I'll be seeing you in the morning."

"Yeah, I guess so."

"Aight then, drive safely and stay sexy."

"I will. You stay handsome." They both laughed. Just then, Ty pulled up and rolled the window down.

"Yall better be discussing B.I. and nothing else. Hots, lets go."

Hots jumped in the car and Ty hit the horn. Rockie did the same and put her truck in drive.

---

IT HAD BEEN over 3 weeks and Rockie was feeling herself. Although she felt like she was on top of the world, Rockie was anxious about this Two-Face character. "Everything will be revealed in due time, just be patient Rockie." She said to herself. Until then, she was going to continue to do big things in Far Rock. Rockie's pick up was 10 bricks and she was down to two within a month's span. The day was Friday and Rockie had just finished a little homework. After her homework, she thought to call Games to see how he was doing. His phone rang twice before he picked up.

"What's the business boss lady?"

"You bro, sometimes me. Just checking on you to see if you're ok"

"You're right on time. I'ma need at least one by tomorrow.

"Aight then, I'll have Zoe bring that to O.V., call my phone as soon as you wake up, cuz I'll be with my baby."

"You got it! Why hasn't your sister called me today?"

"Now you know better Games. We're twins and all, but you know that girl is a book worm or she's out shopping."

"That is why I love her, what more can a man ask for? If you speak to her before I do, let her know I'm in the streets. As soon as I get in the house, I will hit her phone.

"Ok, you do that, LOVE."

"LOVE." Games replied.

After Rockie hung up with Games, her phone began ringing. Drakes song 'You the best I ever had', was her ringtone for G-money.

"Hey babe"

"How you doing my future?" G-money asked.

"I'm good. I was just about to call your phone, what we looking like?" Rockie asked him.

"Raquel, Now you know this is our night and nothing could ever be that important."

"Ok babe, I'm finishing up my homework as we speak. Once I am done, I'm going to hop in the shower and pack an overnight bag."

"That will work. We are going to New Roc City tomorrow, so drive the truck over here. I'm about to head home now. I bought Diamond some new shit to rock tomorrow and she's been calling me since school let out."

"Ok G-baby. I will call your phone when I am close. Love you."

"Love you more." They hung up and Rockie began getting herself together.

# CHAPTER 25

D-nice was laying in the bed at his shorty's crib. She was more like a jump off to D-nice. The fact that she got his cracks off while he was gone, made him dig her even more. It got to the point he would leave packs there and she dumped them for him. He had a little respect for her because every dime was there, every single time. D-nice sparked a blunt that was mixed with sour and haze, as Maliah was making his plate. Her mother made some fried pork chops with rice and beans.

"D, I don't know why my mother cooked this shit, so I had to check to see if she was sick."

"Leave ya momma alone and come feed me some of that good shit."

"It's very hot. Let it sit for a sec." Maliah said while placing it down on the dresser.

"Ma, you know I like it hot. That food can wait. Give me some of that good shit stuff." D-nice took a deep pull of the blunt, as Maliah crawled up on the bed. She took his dick out his pants and started giving him head.

"Shit, it gets no better than this. I get to eat good and get my dick sucked, all while making about $1,500 a night. This is the good life." D-nice thought to himself. Maliah gave him head for the next 20 minutes before D-nice nutted in her mouth without a warning.

"You always do that D-nice." She said after swallowing every drop.

"I bet you ready to eat now, hungry ass." She passed him his plate while she went to the bathroom. While D-nice was eating and watching his favorite cartoon "Dragon Ball Z", a loud bang on the house door startled him. He put his plate on the floor and grabbed his brand-new Desert Eagle from under the pillow.

"Nigga wont you calm down." Maliah said while getting up to see who was banging on her door. Only one person was known to bang like that besides the police and that was her brother Carlos. The streets called him Los. However he was locked up. He received a two-year sentence getting caught with a gun. Maliah had no idea when he was due to come home, so she would have never guessed it was him at the door. When she opened the door, Los was standing there with an attitude.

"What the hell took you so long?" he said. He pushed his 210-pound frame through the door. Los was only about 5'10" maybe 5'11" in height, so he was type big. With a scar on his face, his short curly fro and his green eyes, he was not all that bad looking.

"What's good bro?" you just like popping up on us, huh?"

"Ma knew I was coming home today. That's why it smells like my favorite in this bitch."

Now Maliah knew why her mother cooked this meal. Shit, her mother had not cooked in over a month.

"Well, can I get some love nigga? You acting like your baby sis ain't standing here."

Los picked her up and gave her a big hug.

"Damn girl, you got big in just two years. Aight, now go fix a nigga a plate. I'ma go wash my hands. Where the hell mommy at anyway?"

"I think she's downstairs at Ms. Ann's house."

Maliah went to make her brother a plate while he washed up. When Los walked out the bathroom from washing his hands, he noticed Maliah's bedroom door cracked. He peeked inside. Los could not believe a nigga was laying in his lil' sister's bed.

"Yo nigga, who the fuck is you?" Los asked.

D-nice jumped up with his gun in hand pointing it at Los.

"Nigga, who the fuck are you?"

When Maliah heard the commotion, she ran to her bedroom. When she walked in, she screamed at D-nice.

"No D! That is my brother, just chill."

She stood in front of her brother, while D-nice put his gun down.

"Yo, my fault son. Why didn't you tell me you had a brother Maliah?"

Maliah calmed her brother down and got him to go to the kitchen. They sat at the kitchen table and caught up on things.

"So you really think you a big girl, huh?"

"I have been holding me and mommy down since you been gone."

"And how you was doing that?" Los asked.

"Never mind all that. I also wanted you to know ya baby boy G-money, got all big headed out here. He disrespected me outside in front of people and he put his hands on me."

"He did what? Nah, G-money don't give it up like that, especially knowing your my lil' sis. If it were not for that dirt we put in together, he wouldn't be in the position he is in now."

"I know. Trust me I know, but he acts like he forgot. He said he don't give a fuck who I tell and all this fly shit."

"Word, we will just see about all of that. Tell your boyfriend to come out here and let me holla at him."

Maliah went to get D-nice.

"Yo what's good bro?" D-nice asked.

"Ain't shit. I hear you're not from the Fern, so where you from?"

"I'm really from upstate, Da Roc, but I moved to O.V. last year."

"Aight Rochester. Yeah man, I was up top with a few homies from Da Roc."

Los and D-nice chopped it up for about an hour. D-nice learned a lot about Los and his life in Red Fern. Los mentioning how him, and G-money put in work to take over Red Fern, stuck out like a sore thumb. For G-money to disrespect and act a fool with his sister seemed crazy. Los asked D-nice if he could hold a hammer. He promised he would hit him off when the time was right. Los also asked D-nice if he was pushing heavy work. He explained how he could help double it, seeing as without a doubt, that Red Fern belonged to him. They discussed numbers amongst other things before D-nice told Los he'll get back at him.


THE NEXT DAY G-money woke up to kisses on his face.

"Ahh shit, what are you trying to do to a nigga." He asked.

"I'm just waking you up before you sleep all day. Shit, the way you sexed me last night, I thought I'd still be asleep."

Rockie said with a smile.

"Well, why aren't you?"

"I had a bad dream. We were living together and had a big fight. You packed all your stuff and left. The next day, I received a call saying you had been shot, and might not make it."

"You know I'm not never going to walk out on you. Now I might have to go take a walk, but then again, I'll make you take it." They both laughed and Rockie threw one of her famous jabs. "Ouch, you always hooking me, don't be surprised when I hook back."

"The element of surprise only works when you're not on point....that I will always be!"

"You always talking some fly shit. Get up, I have to use the bathroom. While G-money was in the bathroom, his phone started to ring. Rockie picked up his phone to take it to him. She tried to push through the door, but G-money would not let her in.

"Ma, what are you doing? Can't you see I'm pissing?"

"I know that, but your phone is ringing."

"Aight. Well answer it or let that shit ring."

When Rockie decided to answer, the caller hung up. The caller called right back.

"Hello." Rockie answered in her sexy voice.

"Who the hell is this? Halle Berry or something? And where is G-money?" Dre asked.

"First of all, that is not how you call someone's phone. Second, thanks for the compliment, now hold on." Rockie said. G-money was brushing his teeth when Rockie passed him the phone. Spitting out the toothpaste, he asked "Who is it?"

"I don't know. It's not one of your hoochie mommas, that I do know."

G-money started talking to whoever was on the phone.

"Yo."

"Nigga, who the hell was that sounding crazy sexy?" Dre asked.

"Watch your shit lil' homie. That is my future! What's good though?"

"Check it, I'm done with that. I need you to drop something off to me before you get into your day."

"Aight, give me 20 minutes, but be outside. I don't feel like coming upstairs."

"I'll be in front of the building. Oh, before I hang up let me tell you.... guess who's home?" Dre asked.

"Nigga who? I ain't trying to play no guessing game."

"That nigga Los!"

"Word! My son is home and haven't got at me yet? I will check him tonight. I have plans with the family today."

"Aight, well I'm waiting."

When G-money hung up, Rockie was looking at him funny.

"Where do you think you're going?"

"I'm just dropping something off really quick. By the time I get back, you and Diamond should be ready. We are going out to have brunch.

"Yeah, whatever!" Rockie said as she went into the bathroom to shower. Before G-money left out, he crept in the bathroom and threw cold water into the shower at Rockie.

"Surprise." G-money yelled.

"I'ma kill you Glen!" Rockie yelled back.

G-money kissed his mother and lil' sister before walking out the door.

Los was standing on the corner of Hassock street, using the pay phone. He was leaving Nitty a message, after being sent to voicemail. When Los hung up, he walked into the store to buy a pack of Newport's and a Snapple Apple. After paying for his stuff and pocketing his change, he cracked his pack of Newport's and lit one up. He opened his Snapple, took a sip, and quickly closed it. Los could not believe his eyes.

G-money was double parked across the street, leaning up against a red Range.

"This nigga luck just ran out." Los said to himself.

Los threw his Snapple in the garbage can and pulled out the 380 Glock he got from D-nice. He cocked it and began crossing the street. Dre peeped Los coming across the street, as he walked towards G-money. Dre threw his hands up at Los.

"Yo Los, what's good boy?"

G-money turned around and saw Los with a gun in his hand. G-moneys natural instincts was to reach for a gun. In that quick moment, he realized it was inside the truck. That slip up caused G-money to get hit with the first shot. He fell to the ground and grabbed his shoulder where the bullet went in and out. Dre pulled out once he saw all of this unfold. Dre let off 3 shots in the direction Los was in, with none of them hitting its mark. Los made it to the driver's side of the Range. He opened the door and climbed inside, while G-money was opening the passenger door.

'"G-money, No!" Dre yelled.

It was too late. As G-money tried pulling himself up, Los had the 380 pointed right at his head. G-money looked dead in his eyes as Los said, "You'll never hit a nigga's sister again."

Dre let off 2 more shots with one hitting Los right in his neck. The impact of Dre's 357 snub nose made Los' body jerk. The jerking movements caused Los to squeeze the trigger of his 380, striking G-money in the head.

Dre got closer to the truck to see Los bleeding to death. He picked G-money up and put him in the back of the truck and then jumped in the passenger seat.

"What the fuck was on your mind Los?" Dre asked as he pushed the driver door open and shoved Los into the streets.

"Bet I know what's on your mind now." Dre said before firing his last shot into Los' skull. He started the truck up and made his way to the closest hospital. Dre dialed Nitty's number and he did not get an answer. He then called Cuba.

"Yo Cuba, I need you to meet me at St. Johns Hospital, G-money got shot."

"Aight, I'm on my way." Cuba said.

"Yo, call G-money's crib and tell his moms to get there quick."

Dre hung up and looked back at G-money who was covered in blood, from his face to his chest.

"Bro, you gone be alright. Just hold on. I got you!"

# CHAPTER 26

Games and Rah Rah were sitting in the park, watching Games nephew ride around in his Escalade Power Wheel.

"How's it going with this Two-Face dude, have you guys made any progress?" Rah Rah asked.

"Nah, Nothing yet. I've waiting for this dude named Nitty to call me, but he hasn't. Fresh used to fuck with Nitty out in Brooklyn."

"I've heard that name before."

"Who Nitty?" Games asked.

"Yeah. I remember my father saying that name before."

"Oh yeah, that's how Fresh began dealing with him. Your pops used to hit him off heavy." Just then Rah Rah had a sharp pain In her stomach. She bent down in pain grabbing her stomach.

"Is it that time of the month" He asked with a smile on his face.

"No! I just got off that. You are funny though.

"Well, are you ok?"

"Yeah, I guess so. It feels like a stomach-ache now"

"Aight, lets take it upstairs." As soon as Games said this, Rah Rah threw up. As she threw up, Games phone started ringing. He ignored it while grabbing baby wipes from his nephews' bag. Games held Rah Rah's face while wiping her mouth.

His phone began ringing again, he picked up this time.

"Yo Games, Niggas seen Rockie's truck out in Red Fern during a big shoot out." D-nice yelled through the phone.

"What! Where the fuck is she? D-nice, find her now, I'm on my way." Games hung up.

"Rah Rah, take lil' man upstairs now. I have an emergency, can you make it?"

"Yeah, I guess so." Games called his sister and told her to come down to help Rah Rah with lil' man.

---

NITTY AND TWO-FACE just left from seeing Mr. Wu. They pulled up to the Pink Houses in Brooklyn. We have to go to Queens today, I gotta pick up this bread from G-money." Nitty said.

"What's up with that nigga? You haven't heard from son in a few days."

"That nigga been with some bitch. He been on his L.L. Cool J shit lately. Matter of fact, let me hit him up."

Nitty picked up his phone and noticed he had a few missed calls and messages. He decided to check them. The first one was from Los. Nitty listened with a smile on his face until Los said "Oh yeah, that nigga G-money, will be sitting next to Swift when I catch him. My sister ain't no punching bag. You'll probably call him and put him on point but fuck it though." He hung up. Nitty, looking puzzled, checked the time the message was left. "11:38 this morning? This nigga Los just came home and bugging out already." He said to himself. His second message was from Dre. Nitty could not believe that Dre called to say G-money had been hit up. When he checked the time of that message it said 12:02 P.M.

"Yo, call this nigga Murda and tell him to come downstairs to pick this shit up. We got to get to Queens, this nigga Los just hit G-money up."

"What? How the fuck...Los is home? Two-Face asked confused while calling Murda. Murda came down to grab the work Nitty had. After the drop-off, Nitty and Two-face headed to Queens.

Games sat outside of St. John's Hospital waiting to talk to Rockie. On his way to Red Fern, D-nice called him with the story. Games found himself waiting patiently in the hospital parking lot. Games called Rockie's phone again but hung up when he saw her walking out through the emergency exit. Rockie looked around in the parking lot looking for Games. He honked the horn, making it easier for her to find him. Games could tell she had been crying non-stop from the look on her face. Before she could get to the truck, Games got out and hugged her tight.

"Is he ok?" Games asked.

"Yeah, he'll be alright. He lost a lot of blood from getting shot right underneath his collar bone. The graze to his head left him unconscious because his body went into shock."

"Why you never told me it was G-money you were dealing with all this time? I've been talking to you about the situation out in Red Fern." Games gave her a quick rundown about the entire Red Fern situation.

"Ok, I understand all of that, but what does it have to do with today?" Rockie asked.

"Nothing really, but the dude that shot him, used to be his mans. The dude just came home yesterday. G-money supposedly disrespected his sister in some manner, and homie wasn't having it." Games explained. They talked for a few more minutes until Rockie told Games she would call him later.

ROCKIE WAS SITTING in the waiting room with G-money's mother when she started feeling lightheaded and nauseous.

"Are you ok Raquel?" Ms. Sanchez asked.

Rockie could not answer her as her head began to pound and heart began to race. All Rockie could do was bend over in her chair. Ms. Sanchez called for a nurse. Two came running in their direction before asking what was wrong. Ms. Sanchez explained that Rockie was her daughter and was not feeling well. As they stood Rockie up, she almost threw up on one of the nurses. Luckily, the nurse moved out the way. The nurses took her to a room and began examining her.

When Rockie woke up, her real mother and twin were right by her side. Rah Rah stood beside her and started rubbing her arm as their mother was resting in the hospital chair.

"Twin, are you ok?" Rah Rah asked.

"I'm thirsty as hell." Rockie said in a dry tone.

Rah Rah went to pour her some water when their mother woke up from her nap.

"So you're finally up, huh?" Latasha asked.

"Yeah, I guess so. What am I doing in the hospital Ma?"

"Let's just say, somebody missed their little friend and now you're paying for it."

Rockie almost choked on the water that was given to her. Latasha sat her up and patted her back.

"Ma, are you serious?"

"As a heart attack. How didn't you realize that you missed your period, Raquel?"

"Ma, I don't know. It's been a lot going on in the last month or so."

"I see. Just know you have a lot of explaining to do miss lady when you get home." Latasha said in a stern tone.

"Is Glen ok? Is his mother still here?" Rockie asked. "Yes, your baby father is fine. His mother went home to tend to her daughter. She said she'll be back in the morning."

"Do I have to really sit in here? I need to see him. And besides, I don't feel like I should be in here, I feel fine."

"I'll tell the doctor you're up." Rah Rah offered. Once the nurse came and checked on Rockie's vitals, she was free to leave. Rockie left the hospital with the news that she was 8 weeks pregnant. She could not tell G-money just yet because visiting hours were over. Latasha and Rah Rah took Rockie home for some much-needed rest. When they got home, Rockie went up to her room to see that someone had straightened up. The first thing she did was look in her closet for her Louis Vuitton overnight bag. It was not at the bottom of the closet where she left it. Panic began to set in for Rockie.

"Looking for this?" Latasha asked while standing in the bedroom doorway with the Louis bag in her hand.

"Ma, what are you doing with that?" Rockie asked.

"The question is, what are you doing with it?" Not allowing Rockie to answer, Latasha continued. "Not only are you fucking and pregnant, but you're dealing drugs too? All while you are still under my roof? You got a lot of shit with you Raquel!"

Never hearing her mother speak this way, Rockie knew she was beyond upset.

"Raquel, you don't want or need for nothing...you hear me? Nothing! So why? Sit down Raquel and talk to me." Latasha said with tears in her eyes.

Rockie sat down next to her mother on the bed. She began to explain her madness to her. Rockie was so devoted and passionate about her plan, Latasha felt as if it was Swift talking to her. Latasha overstood how much Swift meant to the twins, she also understood what they were feeling. They spoke on it many times. The twins always felt as if Swift's killer was still out there. Rockie explained what her goals were and how dedicated she was to them to her mother.

Latasha turned to her and looked her square in the eye

"Raquel, you seem like you have your mind made up. Now look here, I will not fuss or fight with you. All I ask is that you allow me to coach you. Let me teach you, what your father taught me."

Rockie never expected her mother to be this understanding, let alone so supportive. She accepted her mother's terms and gave her a big hug.

"Now, what about what's baking in the oven?" Latasha asked.

"Ma, I promise to not let this affect me graduating. I am going to do what is right and hold it down. You did it, right?"

"I sure did! And I believe in you, so make me not only a proud mother, but a proud grandmother. I got your back girl."

They hugged for about 10 minutes while letting the tears fall.

# CHAPTER 27

Zoe was on his way to pick up Rockie when his phone rang. He picked up on the second ring.

"Boss man what's up?"

"Ain't shit Zoe, how you doing?" Asked Hots

"I'm on my way now to pick up Boss lady. She has to go to the hospital and from there we are going to pick up her truck."

"Alright cool. Just keep things together. She is not to deal with Red Fern at all right now, they are watching those projects."

"You got it Boss man."

"Remember, if anything happens to that girl, everything in Queens will feel it."

"I'm with you Boss man" Zoe agreed with everything Hots said.

"Aight, call me a little later. One more thing before I go, nobody is to know that we are connected. Copy?"

"Copy." Zoe nodded his head. Zoe was pulling into the driveway of Rockie's home when he hung up. He hit the horn twice and waited for her to come out.

NITTY AND TWO-FACE walked into G-money's hospital room while Pusha and Dre was in there. They gave each other dap and said their what ups. Nitty walked up to G-money's bed.

"What the fuck is up with you G, how you and this nigga come down to this?"

"Man, that lil' nasty freak bitch sister of his started all this shit. Bitch was made a nigga didn't wanna fuck her dirty ass." G-money explained with an attitude. He was more upset at the fact that Nitty came into his room questioning him. "Well you know behind that shit , you have to lay low. The FEDS is all through Red Fern with all this bullshit going on." Nitty said.

"Yo Pusha, Dre, can ya give me a second?" Dre and Pusha stepped out the room to give G-money his privacy.

"Yo Nitty, I don't appreciate you coming up in here coming at me like this, especially in front of my team. I'm laying in a hospital bed because that coward of a nigga could not step to me as a man. We're supposed to be a team, but you acting like you got here on your own."

"Listen G. My connection with ole boy put us here. I respect that you are not afraid to murder to get to the top. That is why I put you in charge of the Queens thing, let us not forget who runs this operation now."

As soon as Nitty finished his last sentence, Rockie walked in with G-money's favorite, McDonalds. When Nitty turned to see Rockie walking in, he could not believe his eyes. He played it cool.

"Hey babe, I brought you your favorite." Rockie said as she walked around the other side of the bed to kiss him. She said hello to Nitty and Two-Face and introduced herself.

G-money tried cutting in, but Nitty helped with the issue that he saw coming.

"Yo G, we will definitely holla at you when you outta here. Two-Face, lets get up out of here."

Once the name Two-Face left Nitty's mouth, Rockie dropped

the soda she was taking out the bag. "Ahh shit, my bad babe. Don't worry, I'll get it."

She spilled a little on G-money. As she bent down to pick up the cup, she took a good look at the short dude with long dreads.

"Yo Nitty, I'll call you when I get out of here, so stay close to ya phone."

Nitty and Two-Face walked out the door. When Rockie knew they were gone, she spoke.

"You knew that nigga Two-Face all this time Glen?"

G-money knew she was upset, it was not often she called him by his real name.

"Yeah, I know the dude. Why what is up? What's the big deal?" As soon as the question left his mouth, he knew.

"Are you serious Glen? That nigga killed my uncle."

"Raquel calm down." G-money raised his voice at her, which he never did before. He moved the wrong way, hurting his shoulder. He grabbed it with his hand.

"Shit!"

"I'm so sorry babe, I didn't mean for you to hurt yourself."

"It's ok, I'm good. Listen my future, I will be on top of that as soon as I am released out of here. I won't let anyone get away with bringing pain to your heart."

"I understand babe, but this is something I have to handle on my own. I'm bout to call my goons and handle this shit now."

She began walking toward the door.

"Raquel!"

She stopped in her tracks and turned to G-money.

"I know, we're having a baby" Rockie rubbed her stomach, thinking about her unborn child and man she loved.

"Please allow me to be the man that will protect you with his life, if need be. I will not be able to live with myself if anything were to happened to you or our baby. The best I can do is show you that my Loyalty Over Values Everything."

This got Rockies attention and she walked back to his bed.

"Glen, how the hell do you know those two dudes? That other dude is Nitty, he was at my uncle's funeral."

"Don't worry baby. We will connect the dots together. I promise you that. Now tell me about out little man."

G-money said as he pulled her over to the bed and began rubbing her stomach.

"How do you know it's a boy and not a girl?" Rockie teased.

Before he could answer, the door opened and Dre and Pusha walked in. G-money introduced them to Rockie, and they began talking about her having a baby.

---

NITTY WAS TELLING Two-Face that it was time for G-money to go, as they sat in his Benz smoking a blunt.

"Then who's going to hold Red Fern down?" Two-Face asked.

"I'll just have Pusha and Dre hold it down."

"Nigga, you know they gone ride for G-money."

"Not if we make it look like some other niggas did it. Fuck that nigga, he fucking with Swift's daughter! How dangerous is that? How the fuck did it happen anyway?"

"Come on, They're not too far from one another. They could have easily met on the humble. But I can dig it, he should know who she is." Two-Face said.

"He do know! That little nigga up to something, you see how he talking?" Nitty asked him.

"Aight, so what's the plan then? I mean, I already know we have to bring some BK niggas out here."

"Or maybe not Two-Face. I still fucks with the boy Slime from Edgemere. He would be more than willing to earn a few stacks, or I could throw him half a bird. I think I will give him a call when we get back to Brooklyn. Let us take care of this work first." Nitty started his car and headed out to Brooklyn.

ZOE AND ROCKIE pulled into her mother's driveway. She looked around and could tell no one was home yet. They both exited the truck. Zoe walked to the back of the truck and grabbed Rockie's bags. Rockie carried her Gucci purse and a grocery bag full of Rum Raisin ice cream and big bags of Sour Cream & Onion potato chips. They walked into the house while Rockie asked Zoe questions about what she learned today. "Just know this boss lady, whatever it is that you decide to do, I'm with you. And if I am with you, then you got an African Tribe with you."

They both began laughing. Rockie started to put away some groceries she picked up for her mother, she turned to Zoe and asked, " You think I should call Hots or Ty with this?"

"That's all up to you boss lady. I am sure you can handle this though. If G-money says he's dealt with these dudes, then it should be easy."

"You're right Zoe. What was I thinking? I got this and I'm going to show them that I do." Rockie said with more confidence than a little bit.

"Now where the hell is my under boss?" Rockie was referring to Games, who was supposed to be meeting her and Zoe at the house.

"He called when you were in the store getting your goodies. He said he'll be right behind us."

No sooner than Zoe spoke those words, Games pulled up with Dro. They were all seated downstairs in the basement where Rockie sat in her Father's old Lazy Boy. It gave her the feeling as if she were in control and like the boss her father was. As Zoe and Games rolled up some sour, Dro gave everyone a glass with some Henny in it.

"None for me." Rockie said while pushing the glass away.

"Now you know she can't be drinking." Games said

As the blunts were sparked, Rockie began explaining the information she recently found out. They listened with hate boiling in their blood. Games wanted to round up a team as soon as Rockie was done. Rockie also explained how this would be taken care of, she wanted everyone to act accordingly. As she went through her plans, the fellas smoked and sipped. When Rockie asked if anyone had a problem or questions, everyone declined.

# CHAPTER 28

Two-Face and his boy Murda were putting the last bit of their plan together. Two-Face rolled up and lit a blunt mixed with Haze and White Widow.

"Oh, I can't smoke none of this shit. Not right here before the job. This shit could put a nigga in a coma." Murda was saying after taking a pull of the blunt.

"So you understand everything right?" Two-Face asked.

"Nigga, what is there to understand? When you and homeboy is chopping it up and after the transaction is made, I come out and put two in his melon."

"Yeah all that, but you have to be careful doing this. We're headed out there and I'm sure he's going to have someone watching his back. We'll be meeting in front of the McDonald's and it's too out in the open to make a move. Who's our getaway driver?" Two-Face asked.

"I got speedy on the job."

"Man, that nigga a dope fiend!" Two-Face shouted.

"Yeah, but that's when he's at his best. Listen dog, I've seen this dude in action, so don't worry about that." Murda said.

"Aight then, get this nigga over here so I can holla at him. We have to be on the same page."

Nitty called Two-Face on his cell phone to check up on things. He let Two-Face convince him into handling this problem, which he didn't feel comfortable with at all. Once Two-Face explained it to him, it made sense. The plan was to send Two-Face for the job. If they sent anyone else to meet up with G-money, it would look suspicious.

"What's good Nitty?" Two-Face answered.

"What's good with you? You know I had to check up on you, see if everything is correct."

"Yeah, everything is good. I'ma pick up those toys tonight, so we'll be ready by tomorrow."

"Do that, because I want yall to be up and ready when I give you the call."

"Aight Nitty. I'll hit you back once I've picked everything up. I might take it down early tonight." They both hung up.

Two-Face finished his blunt with Murda and broke out to handle his business.

———

IT HAD BEEN a week since G-money was discharged from the hospital. All G-money could do was lay up with Rockie. She wouldn't let him do anything, especially by himself. Rockie explained to how it was a good idea for him to lay low and stay with her for a while. She told him to convince his mother to take Diamond and get out of Queens for a minute. There was too much going on and she didn't want anything to happen to them. G-money got his mother to pack a few things for her stay in Harlem with his grandmother. G-money laid in the bed watching a basket-ball game on ESPN. Rockie walked in with a plate of food.

"You want some babe?"

"Yeah, I should eat some of that with you, we wouldn't want you blowing up like a balloon."

G-money winced in pain. His shoulder hurry here and there.

His facial expression prompted Rockie to bring him some pain killers.

"Here, take these pills and stop talking shit before I punch you in that bad shoulder. And if I do blow up like a balloon, you better still love me. This all your fault anyway."

Rockie took the first bite then fed G-money some.

"So are you ready for tomorrow?" Rockie asked.

"Of course, my future. I'm always ready. This is the perfect chance. I'm glad Nitty wanted to send Two-Face to make the drop off."

"Babe, do you think Nitty knows what's going on or even what Two-Face did to my uncle." Rockie asked.

"We shall find out, but there's no guarantee. I'm sure it will show or come out after this."

They talked about the situation at hand while they ate. Once they were finished, they laid down to get much needed rest.

G-money woke up to the pleasant aroma of bacon, eggs, grits with cheese and pancakes. This put a big smile on his face.

"Good morning G-baby." Rockie said while entering the room. She climbed on the bed to kiss him.

"Morning good." Was his response.

"Well get up and brush your face and wash your teeth, mommy has breakfast ready." They both laughed at her and her jokes. "Yes, my future. I'ma take care of all that and get downstairs to stuff my face. I see you wasted no time feeding your face though." He said while wiping syrup from the corner of her mouth. G-money made his way downstairs and said good morning as he kissed Latasha and Rah Rah. "It smells like Grandma's kitchen in here." He said.

"Well thanks to you, that's exactly what it is." Latasha said in a sarcastic tone then cracked a smile. Everyone started laughing. G-moneys phone went off during the laughter. He saw it was Nitty and answered quickly.

"What's good big man?"

"Just checking up on you to see if your ready for me." Nitty said.

"I told you I was ready a few days ago, but my shoulder has been killing me. Nevertheless, I'm meeting up with your partner at 1 P.M., correct?"

"Yeah, its all set up. But yo check it, I'ma only have one instead of two. I'll get the other one to you, later in the week." Nitty only said this to see how G-money would respond. G-money didn't act on it at all.

"Aight, not a problem. I still got the whole 60." After agreeing on everything they hung up. G-money started eating his breakfast.

Games and Dro pulled up to Rockies house and got out the car. Rockie, Zoe and G-money were standing in the driveway discussing their plans. Games walked up, gave Zoe dap and Rockie a tight hug. "LOVE, baby girl." He said to Rockie. He then gave G-money a nod, G-money gave him one in return. Dro repeated Games' actions. There was an awkward silence until Rockie said something.

"Listen, this cannot go on between the two of you. I know there's bad blood between yall, but it must be put to rest. We are all on the same team now, and we all have common goals. Now can we get down to business? We only have an hour and ten minutes before show down."

Just then, Dre and Pusha pulled up in a black charger.

"Just on time." G-money thought. They all went over what needed to be done before taking off to their destination.

ZOE AND ROCKIE sat parked a block before McDonalds. Rockie had her walkie-talkie in her hands, it was connected to the earpieces she gave to everyone.

"Everybody in position, we're just waiting on Two-Face."

"You see that black Impala parked across the street?" Zoe asked while pointing his finger in the direction of the car.

"Yeah, I see it. It's been sitting there for a minute."

"Well, I got my eye on it because someone's in it."

Meanwhile Games and Dro were in position directly across the street from the McDonalds entrance. Games and Dro were to snatch Two-Face up as soon as he exited McDonalds. Dre and Pusha were in the McDonalds parking lot, just incase anything was to pop off. They sat in a stolen black Charger, each of them had two Tech 9's ready to do whatever.

When Two-Face pulled up to the McDonalds, he pulled up in a white G37 Infiniti Coupe. He waited for an older black man with two kids, to pull out from a parking space. Two-Face pulled into the spot as the family drove off. The entire time, he was unaware that Rockie was on the phone with

G-money. She was letting him know every move Two-Face made.

"Baby, I see him. I picked a table right by the window. That way, Games can see when dude walks out. He can bust that U-turn before he get out the store. Just relax baby and watch my back, lets get off this phone. Here he comes."

G-money knew this situation was about to get ugly. He could not let Two-Face mutter two words. That would be dangerous if he did. Exactly 10 minutes later, Rockie and Zoe watched G-money and Two-Face walking out of McDonalds.

"Where the hell is he going?" Rockie asked herself.

G-money was not supposed to leave out of McDonalds.

"Games get over there." Rockie screamed through her walkie-talkie.

"Look at this shit, who the fuck is this nigga?" Zoe asked. He was referring to the dude getting out of the Impala's passenger side. It was Murda. He wore a blue Champion pull over hoodie and was walking towards McDonald's.

"It's a set up, get in there." Rockie screamed while opening the door to get out. Zoe grabbed her arm. "Boss lady, I can't let you go out there. I got this. Now close that door and get behind the wheel."

He was right, and Rockie knew it. Zoe pulled out a 44 Bulldog while hopping out the car. Murda threw his hood on and walked diagonally toward his prey. He was so focused, he didn't notice Zoe was about 20 feet behind him.

Murda pulled out two 16-shot 9's as he got closer to Two-Face and G-money. When he was about 10 feet away from his target, he began squeezing from both guns. Two-Face was reaching into the back seat of the Infiniti as the first shot went off. He tried to come up with the Mac 11 he had stashed in the back seat. G-money became skeptical once Two-Face said the work was in the car, and the both of them had to get it. Two-Face signed his death certificate the moment Murda started shooting. G-money ran up behind Two-Face before he could come up with that Mac and put two shots in his dreads. G-money jumped inside the back of the car to get away from Murda's bullets. Murda was able to get a few shots off. Once Zoe got close enough, he took aim and hit Murda in the back twice. The impact from the 44 Bulldog sent Murda flying forward. Dre just so happened to be doing 40 mile per hour out of the parking lot. Murda's body flew right into his path, hitting the hood of the stolen Charger. Dre stopped short and Pusha hopped out to make sure Murda was dead. Pusha hit him once in the head and got back in the Charger. Dre hit the horn to let Zoe know, Murda was a wrap. Zoe tucked the Bulldog in the pocket of his black Champion zipper hoodie, while Dre and Pusha got up outta dodge. Zoe ran to the passenger side of his truck and got in. Rockie was parked right behind, Games who was parked right next to Two-Face's white Infiniti. Dro and

G-money searched the car up and down. They were looking for the drugs Two-Face was supposed to deliver but came up empty.

"Alright, let's go. I hear sirens. Let's go!" Rockie yelled.

Dro jumped in with Games, while G-money got in the back of the truck with Rockie and Zoe. On the ride back to Rockie's house, she questioned G-money on what took place back there.

"What happened, G-baby? What made you come out?"

"Baby, he didn't bring the product. He asked me to go to the car with him to get it. I couldn't say no without looking suspicious."

"It was set up anyway. But why, why would they be out to kill you?"

"Your guess is as good as mine, but we know Nitty's behind all this bullshit. Brooklyn niggas!" G-money said in a mumbled tone.

"Yeah, I agree. Nitty needs to be snatched up. As a matter of fact, behind all this shit, he won't be out in the open. He'll hide, once he knows that we know."

They all sat in silence in their own thoughts. G-money thought about revenge against that bitch ass nigga Nitty. Rockie wanted to know why it seemed Nitty wanted everyone she loved dead. Zoe was busy trying to put all the pieces of the puzzle together in his head.

# CHAPTER 29

Nitty was sitting in his living room, smoking a blunt and drinking Henny straight out the bottle. He was thinking about Two-Face and was fucked up about it. Nitty had been drinking and in his feelings for the past two days. When speedy came back to his place, without Two-Face or Murda, he knew what took place. He wanted to kill Speedy right there on the spot but knew that would be stupid. Especially after listening to the whole story. Speedy explained how it all went down and Nitty couldn't believe it. The way the whole incident unfolded left Nitty speechless. Nitty knew G-money had every intention of killing him, Two-Face or whoever showed up, once hearing speedy out.

"That's why I wanted him dead from the jump. He was getting too big for himself." Nitty thought. Nitty tried to understand why G-money wanted him dead.

"Just greedy I guess."

Nitty planned to lay low for a moment. While laying low, he would create a plan to get G-money out the way for good. The first thing he did was call up a few of his Brooklyn Knights, and then holla at Slime from Edgemere.

IT HAD BEEN a little over a week since G-money killed Two-Face and he could not get it out of his mind. He never had this type of problem. G-money knew where it was coming from. It was his guilty conscience. Being in love with Rockie, knowing she was Swift's daughter played heavy on his mind.

G-money never had a problem killing a man before, but this whole situation was killing him. He kept seeing Two-Face and his dreads, covered in blood. G-money was sitting in the tub, relaxing his muscles and his nerves. He sipped on some Henny out of a glass as the water began to get cold. Rockie walked in the bathroom.

"G-baby, how long are you going to sit in this tub? I know the water is cold by now."

"It's alright." He said never looking up. "But I'm about to get out now, just needed some time to think and relax."

"Are you still thinking about Nitty?" Not waiting for a response she continued.

"Don't stress yourself with that G-baby. My people are on it. Right now he's hiding, but he can't do that for too long."

"Yeah, I guess you're right." He said getting up and out the tub. He grabbed a towel and wrapped it around his waist.

"Yeah, cover that thang up." Rockie said with a smile.

He knew she was trying to lighten the mood.

"Now can we just go to bed? I have to get up for school in the morning." She said in a demanding tone. G-money didn't reply, he just walked behind Rockie into the bedroom. He threw his boxers on and then grabbed the T.V. remote. As he got into bed next to Rockie, he turned the T.V. on.

Never expecting to see what just popped up on the screen, he tried to change the channel. With Rockie laying next to him, he surely didn't want her to see it. It was too late though. Rockie nudged him, saying "G-baby, I know you saw that turn back."

Without an argument, he flipped the channel back. They both watched and listened in awe.

"Glen Sanchez is wanted for two murders in the city of Queens. He is also having conspiracy charges for other murders in the city of Queens. He's...." G-money turned the channel before 'America's Most Wanted,' showed the pictures of the two men he murdered.

"Why did you do that?" Rockie asked.

"My future, there's no reason to watch something that will only complicate things."

Rockie began telling him she would call her peoples to see if they could help. She ended their hour-long conversation by telling him how much she loved him and how she needed rest.

G-money did not know how close he was to being exposed, but he felt it. That was the real reason he turned the channel. The fact that he didn't know who else might have seen the program, worried him. G-money promised Rockie he would stay in the house, until she came home from school. This was becoming too much to hide. As he forced himself to fall asleep, he thought about Nitty. He had to get to Nitty, and fast.

The next morning, Rah Rah felt like driving herself and Rockie to school. She wanted to discuss Rockie's safety. She was afraid that something might happen to Rockie with everything going on.

"I'm really scared for you out here, Raquel. All of this is becoming too much."

"I'll be fine Rah Rah. Once I get Nitty, I will have my baby, open a small business, finish high school, and then live happily ever after. This is not something I am trying to do for the rest of my life. I just want who killed daddy. This money is great, but it's not that important to me. Although I do enjoy it! Tearing up the mall and all." That brought a smile to Rah Rah's face.

"Yeah, that's definitely one of the fun parts. Matter of fact, when are we gone do some retail therapy for that belly of yours?" Rah Rah asked.

"It's been a minute, right? We can go to Jersey. How about Saturday morning, Bet?"

"Bet twin."

---

ZOE WAS on his way to make a drop off to Slime in Edgemere. Zoe used to drive Slime around, this is how they became cool peoples. Once he told Slime he had it for the low, he had gained a loyal customer. While Zoe was driving, he was on his cell phone with Hots.

"I'm hearing this BK cat is hiding out."

"Yeah, but once he comes out, you will be contacted, ya dig Zoe?"

"I hear you boss man. Let me ask you this... no disrespect, but if you know how to get to this dude then..."

Hots cut him off mid-sentence.

"Check it, if Rockie wants to boss and handle it as she pleases, then so be it. We're going to assist her with anything she ask for, but the keyword is what?"

"Ask! This dude has all the answers to her questions though. Do we really want to take the chance of him getting away?"

"Don't worry about him getting away Zoe. That will never happen. The minute he tries to leave Brooklyn, we'll be on him like flies on shit, ya dig?"

"I dig it."

"Aight then, keep me posted and I'll do the same."

"Copy." Zoe said as he hung up, while pulling into the projects.

Hots was coming from picking up his stepdaughters from school when his cell phone rang. He saw it was Rockie and picked up on the second ring.

"If it ain't Lisa Raye, what up?" He answered.

"Why thank you for the beautiful compliment." She began while blushing.

"May I trouble you with an issue I'm having?"

"I don't see why not but right now I'm with my little ladies. We're coming from school on our way home. So how about we talk about it over something to eat?"

"Who's that daddy?" the eldest asked in a grown tone.

"Summer, this is daddy peoples. Now stop being so nosy."

"Oooh, someone getting told on." Rockie said playfully.

"Mommy knows all of daddy's business, so I got no worries. Now back to B.I., Ms. Raye. Are we on for some dinner?"

"Well, I don't know. You know I have a boyfriend and its obvious you have someone..."

"Listen Rockie, I'm not trying to come between any of that. Now don't get me wrong, since Playa's Club, I've been wanting to get my hands-on Lisa Raye. Had this been under other circumstances, nothing would stop me. I would love to get my hands on Thee, Ms. Raye. The one I have come to know. I am here for you in other ways, so take advantage of it. I know I would." He explained.

"That's cool and all. I'll keep that in mind as I wait for your call."

"So dinner it is, huh?

"Yeah, I guess so...by the way, tell the family I said hi."

Rockie hung up before he could respond.

Hots was walking up the steps with his girls. His thoughts were on Rockie. Had he not been in something so complicated already, he would pursue Rockie. She was kind of young, but that was the fun in it, he thought. His mind snapped back to reality as they reached their floor. His girl was right there waiting at the door.

"Mommy" the girls yelled entering the apartment.

---

ROCKIE'S ATTRACTION to Hots was undeniable and she knew he felt the same way. But Rockie was in love with her first and only love, G-money. As she walked in her house from school, she quickly remembered.

"Raquel, where you been? It's after 5 o'clock ." G-money asked, getting off the couch.

"And Hi to you too! Just so you know, Zoe took me to see about my truck. I think I might sell it and buy something else." She said as she put her Louis nap sack down and went to give him a hug.

"Why didn't you call me at least? You know I've been in this house all day!"

G-money said, still pushing the issue. When he did not hug her back, she became agitated.

"Glen, what's the problem? You act like I'm not out here trying to make shit right for all of us!"

"All that's understandable. Just try to put yourself in my shoes. I'm in here all day, with no phone, no nothing! I was worried sick, thinking something might've happened to you."

Rockie understood his frustration, but none of this was her fault. He was Americas Most Wanted and had to get low.

Rockie explained to him how it was not her fault and that he need to trust her. She was working towards getting him out of New York to Somewhere safer. Rockie walked upstairs to her room.

G-money called for her, but Rockie ignored him, never looking back. As she walked up the stairs, her tears began falling. Just as G-money was about to follow behind her, Rockie's mother walked in from work.

"What's going on in here?" Latasha asked as she sat her suitcase down at the door. When she heard G-money call out for Rockie, she sensed that something was wrong.

"Ain't nothing ma, Just a misunderstanding. That's all."

G-money answered.

"Hhmm, I'll just check with my baby about all that. You sit tight." Latasha said as she went up to Rockies' room. When Latasha got to the door, Rockie was in tears. Rockie immediately began to explain the situation with her and

G-money, leaving out nothing. She confessed to Latasha that G-money was a wanted man, which led to the argument they just had. Rockie also told Latasha every detail of the conversation she had with Hots.

"Let me say this." Latasha began

"I am your mother and will always be here for you and support you, the best I can. Now I know you love that boy downstairs, but he must find a place to get low and fast. Because for one, we cannot hide no fugitive in this house. We can all go to jail. Secondly, your heart never lies, so always listen to it. And finally, I have a client for you. Someone your father used to deal with. He's very good peoples and need your help. Now I know you have a lot on your plate right now, but here is his number. Make sure you give him a call."

"When?"

"As soon as you can. I just left work, and he said he'll be waiting by the phone."

"Alright, let me call Zoe. Thank you, Ma."

"That's what I'm here for. Did I tell you my client needs a half a key of coke?" Latasha said as an afterthought. Rockie laughed a little.

"Ma, nobody says it like that."

"Now look here, I'm not into all that bird talk." Latasha said.

They both shared a laugh.

Rockie walked out of her room on her cellphone. She was calling Zoe, to tell him about their mission. He told her he would be there in a half-hour. Once their phone call ended, she told G-money her plans. Rockie was going to see her peoples about getting G-money out of state.

"So I can't ride with you?" he asked.

"I don't think it's a good idea."

"Why not?"

Before Rockie could respond, Latasha walked into the living room and voiced her opinion.

"Glen, you know its not safe for all that. They day you leave this house, you should be heading somewhere safe. You should not be running around in the open to possibly get caught up. How about we have someone pick up your mother and sister? You can spend some time with them here. She explained.

With that, G-money had no choice but to oblige. Rockie was on her way out the door as Zoe pulled up to the house.

"So momma love got you checking some of her old peoples?" Zoe asked as they made their way to Manhattan.

"Yeah, something like that. This dude used to deal with my father and works with my mother."

"That means he got that corporate money." Zoe said smiling.

"I guess so." She replied smiling back.

They rode in silence until they were in Downtown Manhattan and Rockie had to call the client.

"Hello." He answered on the first ring.

"Mr. Steven?" she asked,

"Speaking."

"This is Rockie, I'm by Madison Square Garden."

"Ok, I'm in a small restaurant right across the street."

"Alright, I see it. I'll be there in a minute."

"I'm in the back, on the left-hand side."

"Cool." She said then hung up.

Zoe told her he was going to park directly in front of the restaurant. Just in case some funny shit popped off.

Rockie walked towards the back of the restaurant looking like a high school student. She wore a Red Polo V-neck sweater with Burberry Khakis with her matching Khaki colored, 4-inch, Nine West heels. She carried the half a key of coke with books in her Louis Vuitton book bag. The book bag rested on her back, making her look like the schoolgirl she was. A pregnant schoolgirl, as her bell stuck out like a small soccer ball.

"Hello Ms. Raquel." Mr. Stevens greeted her, getting up on his to shake her hand. "Your mother never mentioned you being pregnant." He finished.

"That doesn't really matter. I guess that makes it all better. Let's get down to business." She said shaking the scruffy man's hand. Rockie wasted no time passing him the half a brick under the table. In return, he passed her a brown paper bag that had 15 stacks in it.

"Remember, I'ma need 17/5 for the next one. Or you can get the whole bird for 32." Rockie said as she placed the brown paper bag in her bookbag.

"You're definitely your..." the man paused, catching himself.

Rockie finished the sentence for him. "...father's child, I am my father's child to the T." Sshe said with confidence as she got up to leave. Hots was calling her phone as she was telling Mr. Stevens, she hoped it was all there.

"Shit." Rockie said to herself while stepping out of the restaurant. She was hoping Hots was not in Queens waiting on her, while she was in Manhattan.

"What's up Hots?" she answered on the fourth ring.

"Damn, I thought you changed your mind for a minute! You ain't trynna whisper at your boy?" Hots asked jokingly.

"Whisper?" she asked as she hopped in the car with Zoe.

"I mean everybody screaming and hollering, so why not do the whispering thing?"

"How cute."

"Not as Lisa Raye." He replied and laughed out loud.

"There you go."

"Nah, I'm joking. Not about how cute you are though. But what's up, where you at?"

"Downtown Manhattan, Zoe brought me out here to check on these fly ass shoes." She lied. Zoe just looked at her and smiled.

"That's good right there, cause I'm on 125th street. Tell Zoe to come to Two Fifth and 8th avenue, I'll be in Popeyes. You want something?"

"You know I do! Some of their good ole chicken and biscuits."

"Aight, now what will the baby be having?" he asked with a smile on his face.

"I can see the smile on your face, but it's cool. He'll have some of their fries. I'll see you when I get there." She said hanging up with a big smile.

"Somebody smiling hard or is that blushing?" Zoe asked.

"Just get us to 125$^{th}$ street and 8$^{th}$ avenue. Hots is in Popeyes waiting on us, nosy." She turned her head to the window, still blushing.

Rockie wasn't supposed to feel like this and she knew it. Despite the physical attraction, her gut was leading her in that direction. The fact remained, Hots was handsome, older and about his business. She thought about this while watching the streets of Manhattan, on her way to 125$^{th}$.

Zoe appeared to be alone as he sat on the opposite side of Popeyes by himself. He enjoyed a two-piece chicken and biscuit mean while talking on his cell phone. Rockie and Hot's sat at a window table, seated across from one another. Rockie and Hots ate as they talked.

"So what you doing down here?" Rockie asked Hots while biting into a breast.

"Had to come check some of the peoples in Harlem. Since I was still out here after contacting you, I figure we could meet in the middle. What other place better than Two-Fifth? And I love me some Popeyes. Hope you don't mind." he explained. Rockie took a mental note of how he explained himself to her.

"Nah, I surely don't mind no chicken, I'm mostly black." She said this while licking the chicken grease off her fingers. The shared a laugh at her antics.

"So what's your story or should I say question? It seems important."

Rockie was happy he got right to it because G-money was the importance to this meeting. Focus is what she fell short of for a moment.

"It's about G-money." She stopped mid-sentence as she stared at the smile that appeared on Hots face.

"What's the smile about?" she asked with confusion.

"Relax, its nothing. I may have caught a quick glimpse of the news this morning. I had a hunch us needing to talk was connected to it. Go ahead, I'm listening."

Hots saw the love in her eyes and listened to the love pour from her heart as well.

Rockie was glad she could tell that he noticed all of it.

With what she sensed from his actions, gave her the thought he wouldn't help. After all, Hots had a thing for her which only complicated things.

Rockie watched Hots take a sip of his soda as he sat back.

Before responding to her, he sat the soda on the table.

"I mean, Ty has a few out of the country joints I can ask about. Myself on the other hand, I have local connections. We talking ATL, MIA maybe even Houston or something."

"Is it because you like me?" She asked seriously.

"Why so serious? Of course I like, why is that a question?"

"Your look said different, so don't front on me Hots."

"I don't understand Rockie. How do I look and why the attitude suddenly?"

"Hots, your look said, '...I really don't care to help ya man, but because I like you...'. I'm not gonna lie Hots you basically hit a nerve." She explained with an attitude.

"Rockie, let me explain something to you. My looks can be one thing, but my heart remains the same. Unless its disrespected or stepped on. That being said, Loyalty does Over Value Everything! Your father wouldn't have it no other way. I wasn't around for how Ty and your pops did it. It was obvious he loved Ty. Your father and Ty had a very strong and powerful connection. Meeting Swift and being around Ty, made it a privilege. Now as far as liking you in that manner, clearly, I do. Shit, you know how many dreams I've had of Lisa Raye? So far in my life, you've been the closest to a Lisa

Raye look alike." He smiled as he took her hands and placed them in his.

"The truth is Rockie, I'm already caught in between two women. Sadly, it is something I do not need. Its unfortunate and painful that I don't have the privilege of pursuing someone such as yourself. So beautiful, young, independent, and more importantly you have a heart like your father. One made of platinum. So instead, every chance I get, I remind you of all those special things you possess."

Hearing Hots explain his feelings for Rockie, made her want to reach over and kiss him. His honesty and loyalty were beyond visible. She could tell he loved her by the words he spoke. Rockie wanted to tell him, she loved him too.

———

BACK IN O.V., D-nice was laid up in some shorty's crib he just met two weeks ago. Games told him she was good peoples and had been living out there for years. Plus, she was an older chick, who had her shit together. D-nice did what he did best and pushed up on her. About a week later, he was being served breakfast in bed, and had fiends knocking on her door. Right now, his breakfast was Pat's juicy lips and the sloppiest head he ever had. D-nice woke up to his dick being swallowed and licked like a tootsie pop and boy did it feel good. Pat was 32, a fucking freak and a top-notch pro when it came to sucking dick. He smacked her round ass, as she poked it up in the air.

"Yeah girl, take all that dick." He moaned.

She came up for air quickly and replied.

"Good morning, pretty boy."

"And a good morning it is!"

As she went back giving him head, D-nice placed two fingers inside her dripping wet pussy. Just as he thought he had found a freak in Maliah, Pat fell into his lap. Literally.

Within five minutes, D-nice was practically begging her to stop. He didn't want to cum before digging in her neatly shaved wet pussy. But she would not let up. D-nice knew he was gonna have a bomb ass nut. He began to fuck her mouth.

"Take all this dick...damn girl." He moaned in pleasure as he pumped in and out of her mouth. Within 60 seconds, he nutted so hard, he could not move afterwards. D-nice was laying down, waiting for his heartbeat to slow down, when his cell phone started ringing. He looked at it and it read 'Private'. He tossed the phone back on the nightstand.

"That might be one of your little shorties." Pat said in a fake jealous tone.

"They wouldn't call private, they no better than that."

He replied. Since Pat was an older woman, she always had a smart-ass mouth. Before she could reply with something smart to say, his phone rang again. For the last few days, he had been receiving private phone calls. Seeing that he was feeling good today and liked how Pat played jealous, he answered.

"Who dis?" he asked.

He was not prepared for the voice that spoke on the other end.

"D, papi?"

D-nice sat up in Pat's bed at the sounds of the familiar voice. Caught off guard he responded.

"Maliah?" he asked startled.

Pat sensed the emotions in his question and got up to use the bathroom. D-nice could not help but to admire Pat's ass and sexy walk. She had a body like the Porn Star, Cherokee D'ass, and even favored the dark chocolate adult entertainer.

"D, what up? I been trying to reach you for a minute now." Maliah whined.

"If it has been you calling private these past few days, then you know why I haven't picked up. Fuck all that though. Where you been at? I've been trying to reach you too. I even stopped by your crib, to learn you don't live there no more."

"D, it's a long story and I was hoping you could come see me, so I can explain."

"Oh yeah? You got a lot of explaining to do then, seeing as you got ghost with my bread and shit." He said with much attitude.

"D-nice, you got to know I love you and would never take or steal from you." She said between soft cries.

"Please, take this address and number down. It's very important that we see each other." She finished.

Not wanting to stay on the phone any longer, he took the info down. D-nice told her he had some important shit to do this weekend. He also told her she should hear from him by Monday, no later than Tuesday."

Before hanging up, Maliah told him she loved him.

"Me too." Was his response, pertaining to loving himself. He smiled at the thought of his arrogancy.

# CHAPTER 30

G ames, D-nice, Dro and Ratley were standing in the middle of O.V., enjoying the nice weather of mid-April.

Now that the weather was breaking, the hood was flooded with hood rats, Bebe's kids and senior citizens.

Games and his peoples did the same thing all year round, no matter the season. So as the blunt mixed with sour and Kush went around, Games took in the better weather.

Games had just got off the phone with Rah Rah and it left a big smile on his face. He was excited because they finally discussed her being ready to spend the night with him. Games knew this only meant one thing, he would finally be able to taste Rah Rah's beautiful virgin insides.

The two have been seeing each other exclusively for last 3 months, and Games had been patiently waiting. He was happier than a fat kid in a Twinkie factory.

"Yo Dro, send that nigga light to the liquor store to get another bottle." Games said, thinking about how nice he wanted to be for tonight.

"Damn nigga, who da lucky joint tonight? Cuz you already on

the second bottle and it's only about 6." Dro asked as if he read his mind.

"Stop being so nosy my nigga." He replied with a big grin on his face.

"I did see Kourtney and them bitches about an hour ago, and she asked did I see you." Ratley butted in, getting in on the scoop.

"Fuck outta here! Yall know that bitch be bugging! I can't deal with her fuckery."

"That's What'cha mouth say." Ratley said while dapping Dro and laughing at the same time.

Dro switched up quick. He turned to Ratley and said.

"Nigga you should be easy, cuz your ass can't even keep a bitch! Not even if niggas tied her to ya back."

Now it was Games turn to laugh.

"He ain't never lied." Games replied through laughter and dapping up Dro.

Just then, Light pulled up on a peddle bike.

"Yo Light, we need you to snatch up a $70 bottle of Grey Goose. And do not forget the big can of Goya pineapple juice, get two." Dro said, passing him the money.

Twenty minutes later, they were opening their second bottle and rolling two more blunts. Halfway through their session, Rah Rah called Games phone back.

"Ri Ri, what up baby?" he answered with his nickname for her.

Rah Rah's identical look to the singer Rihanna, was like a dream come true for Games.

"Nothing much sexy chocolate, just trying to find out where you are." She replied.

Walking out of ear shot from the fellas, Games replied.

" Keep sounding like that and I'll never be hard to find. Just look down in your lap."

"Ooh, You're so fresh! Stop it fresh ass! For real though, where are you? And I hope Dro is close by because VVS is right here."

"Yeah, he's right here. We in the middle of O.V. right now. How about you find a parking space and come meet us in the middle."

"Alright, be there in 5 minutes."

They hung up and D-nice was the first to say something.

"This nigga wide open off of shorty and I bet he ain't smell the pussy yet!" Laughter poured out amongst the friends.

"She's sooo bad! And the pussy....I'm sure it is top of line. It'll be so good, you niggas will wanna be my best friend just because I'm fucking her." Games finished.

There was more laughter between the friends.

"Oh shit" D-nice said out of nowhere. He just remembered he had something important to tell them.

"I knew I had something to tell yall." He finished.

That is until Games interrupted him. "Well, spit it out. No Harlem!!!"

"Maliah called me yesterday while I was at Pat's spot."

"Aight so?" Dro asked.

"Nigga, if you'd let me finish. Anyway, you know da bitch disappeared after that shit with her brother and G-money. She had over 5 stacks and about 2 ounces that belonged to me. Now suddenly, she calls from a blocked number, talking about she would never steal from me. Talking about she love me and all this fly shit. But what got me is, she want me to come check her. Talking about she in Middletown and has something important to tell me."

"Sounds serious, or maybe it's a set up." Dro responded.

"Well I say, take a soldier with you and go see what shorty talking about. Shit, who knows, she might have got pregnant or something like that. All I'm saying is, she still might have that paper." Games explained.

"I got some things to handle today. You know niggas don't do too much on Sunday's." D-nice added.

"The best time is a Sunday. When everybody is resting and relaxing. I say drive out there and see what she talking about. And get that paper back!"

They started laughing.

"Yeah, you owe me a couple dollars anyway." Games shot.

"You too?" Dro asked playfully.

"You niggas ain't saying too much of nothing! What I owe you two niggas" D-nice said while pulling out two stacks of money.

"Do I owe you too nigga?" he asked Ratley playfully as he peeled off a few bills.

Just then, Rah Rah and VVS were walking towards them. Games and Dro got their hugs and kisses. The ladies said their hello's to Ratley and D-nice. They grabbed a seat on the benches.

"So this is what yall doing, getting twisted?" Rah Rah asked in the best ghetto voice she could imitate.

"Not twisted, but nice. It's going to be a beautiful night." Games answered.

"Yeah right."

"After this bottle and these blunts, I'll show you." He replied. They finished smoking and drinking then they all went their separate ways.

---

ROCKIE STEPPED out of the shower and wrapped herself in a Donna Karen bath robe. She walked into her bedroom where G-money was laying butt naked. Between the Henny he drank and the sex-capades with Rockie, he was feeling lazy.

"G-baby, what are you doing? It's your turn to shower."

"I'm chill. I just a little rest." He mumbled.

"Ewww, you're nasty." She replied with a smile. Rockie walked back in the bathroom to retrieve a wet and soapy rag. When she returned, G-money had dozed off. She grabbed his limp dick and began washing him clean of their juices.

"Oh baby, that, that shit feels good." He said with his eyes still closed.

"Oh please, you can't handle no more." She said while stroking his dick with the rag. Rockie began to feel moisture in between her legs as his erection grew in her hand. Rockie grabbed a dry towel that was nearby and wiped him dry. His soft moans were causing her juices to overflow. Her pregnancy done made her hornier and brought the freak out of her. With half a hard on, Rockie had to give into another round. She wrapped her lips around his dick and slowly took him in deep. All 9 ½ inches of G-money poked the back of her throat. The slow head only lasted two minutes. Rockie needed to fill her insides with G-money's dick. She climbed on top of him and guided his dick, inside her wetness. Before G-money knew it, Rockie started riding his dick like she would never see it again.

"Oooh G-baby...you feel so good inside me." she moaned with pleasure. By now G-money was up and gripping Rockies ass cheeks. She rode G-money for the next 10 minutes before they came all over and in each other.

"Dam babe, you really draining a nigga, huh?" he asked. "That's cuz I'm going to miss you and the dick." She answered, placing light kisses on his face. All he could do was hold her in deep thought.

"We won't see each other until I graduate. That's after June." She continued.

"Yeah babe, I'm really fucked up behind this shit. I know one thing, we have to figure out a way for me to be there when you have our baby."

"Don't worry G-baby, your future will have it all figured out when that time comes, I promise." She said with a big smile on her face.

"That's why I love you girl."

"And I love you more." She replied.

After 3 hours of sex and no shower for G-money, they laid down and finally fell asleep. Before falling asleep, Rockie thought about how G-money took the news yesterday.

When Rockie came home from meeting with Hots, She

explained their plan to G-money. Rockie told him he was scheduled to leave Monday evening, she booked a flight to Albuquerque,
New Mexico. G-money was not trying to hear it. He made up all
sorts of excuses on why he couldn't be that far way. And although
she understood, she begged him to go. Rockie could not chance him
going to jail for the rest of his life. Rockie explained to him that
their child being fatherless, was not an option. This would break
her heart. After a few more hours, he finally agreed. But only if she
agreed to visit him as much as possible. After Rockie had the baby,
they planned on buying a house out there. They both liked the idea
and agreed on it. Before their sex session and pillow talk, Rockie
spent most of her day at the Jersey Mall. Rah Rah and VVS tagged
along as Rockie went shopping for G-money and spent close to
$10,000. He had her pickup the $150,000 he had stashed at his
mother's house. Rockie took $100,000 of that and gave it to his
mother, for her and Diamond. She put the rest in her safe even
though G-money would be good.

The baby moved around in her stomach, waking her out of her
sleep. It was still dark outside, but she could tell it was early in the
morning. Rockie got up, put her robe on and headed downstairs to
the kitchen. She looked at the clock hanging on the far wall in the
kitchen. It read 4:45 A.M.

Rockie made a bowl of Raisin Bran, sat at the table, and ate.
Her thoughts began to turn toward her father, and what he would
be doing if alive. Tears started to fall because she knew her life
would be completely different. Right now, she was walking in her
father's shoes. And even though was tough enough to do it, she
second guessed herself. Rockie wondered if her father's shoes were
too big to fill. All she wanted, was to remain her father's baby.

G-money moved around in his sleep and noticed Rockie was
not next to him. After checking the time, he got up to check on her.
As he stepped out the room, the dim light from downstairs got his
attention. He followed the light and found Rockie eating a bowl of

cereal, while sitting at the kitchen table. G-money walked up behind her as quietly as he came down the steps. Once directly behind her, he softly touched her shoulder. Rockie jumped.

"G-baby don't do that, you scared me." She said, now on her feet.

"I'm sorry babe. You scared me when I turned around in bed, and you weren't right next to me."

"As you can see, I woke up needing a snack." She said as she sat back in her seat.

"I see greedy." He replied with a little chuckle. "What's the matter babe? I can see tears in your eyes."

"Nothing much, just had a moment thinking about my father." She said softly while placing her spoon in the bowl.

"If he knew that I was supplying half of Queens and being in this game, while pregnant..." She paused then continued.

"Oh boy!"

"Yeah, I could only imagine. But do not forget, he could also be the proudest father in heaven. At the end of the day, he knows he raised one tough cookie." G-money said as he massaged her shoulders.

"Thanks G-baby."

"Don't thank me, it's what I'm here for. Just remember, ya pops could not be prouder. I mean, you are still getting straight A's and you graduate in June. What more could he ask for?"

"I guess you're right. I know I promised that I will make sure my sister and mother are forever good. I know for a fact he's holding me to that."

"And you're doing everything to keep that promise, so don't beat yourself up. Now finish up that soggy ass cereal, so you can get some rest." He said with a smile.

Rockie finished her cereal and washed out her bowl. When they were back in her room, she reminded him about her appointment. Rockie had a doctor's appointment Monday and G-money said he would be there. He needed too, Monday was his last day of being in New York. It was only right he went to the doctor with her one last time.

# CHAPTER 31

Monday morning came so fast that Rockie nor G-money realized it. That is until Rockie's mother knocked on her door.

"Raquel, Glen, it's a quarter after eight! Get yall butts up before Yall late! Now!" Latasha demanded.

We're up, we're up!" Rockie yelled from her bedroom as she wiped the cold from her eyes.

They both got up and began to get themselves ready.

"I'm off to work and Zoe just called. He said he is on his way. Glen, you bring yourself out here and give me some love." Latasha said from the other side of the door. G-money came out and gave her a tight hug and kiss. They exchanged a few words expressing how they loved and would miss each other.

"Rockie keep me updated." Latasha yelled over her shoulder as she left for work.

Rockie and G-money were showered and dressed by the time Zoe pulled up and was hitting the horn. Rah Rah left out earlier, but not before giving her love to G-money.

G-money carried his Louis Vuitton luggage downstairs to Zoe's truck. Zoe helped with his luggage while G-money was on the phone with his mother.

"Ma take care of yourself and Diamond. I am going to make sure I call as much as I can. And do not you worry about a thing. I'll make sure you get some cash every month to hold yall down."

"Boy, you know your momma gonna gold it down. I keeps me a stash." She said. They laughed, and then she continued.

"You just be safe and take care of yourself. We love you and will miss you daily. We are praying for you, ok? And make sure you call your sister as much as possible."

"I promise ma." He stated.

"Tell Raquel I said to give me a call as soon as she can, kay?"

"Ok ma, I got you. I love you."

"I love you too Glen." She replied and hung up.

After talking to his mother, G-money was having second thoughts. But he also knew it would be too dangerous if he stuck around any longer. Just then, Rockie stole his attention as she walked out the house. He thought he saw a smile on her face, which made her seem happy.

"Not at a time like this." He thought to himself, as he watched her talking on her cell phone.

G-money walked up to her, held his hand out and helped her down the few steps in front of the house. Her smile and beauty, along with her basketball belly, made him quickly think past the jealousy he was feeling. Even with her 4-month belly, Rockie was still beautiful and dressed like a model.

Rockie wore a pair of 3-inch yellow Chanel heels with some blue H&M stretchy jeans, that hugged her pregnant curves. Her white blouse with the right shoulder cut-off, was also from H&M. The April morning breeze let her know, she had made the right decision in wearing her blue jean jacket. Rockie's Chanel jean jacket was made of leather material and had yellow stitching.

"Ok. Cool. So as soon as we are done, I'll call you....later." Rockie said ending the phone call.

"Everything good?" G-money asked.

"Yes babe, of course it is. Now let us go to this doctor's appointment before we're late and miss it."

"I'm going to miss you, my future." He said to her.

Rockie stopped in her tracks.

"And you know I'm going to miss you too. Let me rephrase that." She said while rubbing her stomach. "We'll miss you! As soon as I graduate, we are out there for the entire summer. Hearing that made G-money feel good as they walked towards Zoe's truck.

Rockie said hello to Zoe as G-money helped her into the truck.

"Good morning Boss lady, how's the family today?" Zoe asked.

"Everything ok, I guess." She answered in a disappointed tone. "My baby is leaving today and that's the worse!"

"It'll be aight. Let her know G-money, we gonna gold it down. And yall gonna be a family regardless." Zoe said as

G-money climbed in next to Rockie.

"You already Know." G-money replied, trying to shed light on the situation.

"Aight Zoe, I hope you had your sour, because we're running late. It is almost 10 o'clock.

"Don't worry about that, just strap up and relax." Zoe said as he pulled off.

---

WHEN D-NICE GOT UP, he stared around the unfamiliar room. The clock on the nightstand read twenty after 12 noon. After a few minutes of staring around the room, things slowly started to come back to him. D-nice remembered arriving at Maliah's house out in Middletown, New York. It was after 10 o'clock last night when he got there. He also remembered getting fucked up off two bottles of Cîroc.

"So ya finally up, sleeping beauty." Maliah said as she walked in the bedroom with a glass of orange juice.

"Damn, what the fuck happened last night?" he asked while reaching to accept the glass of juice. Maliah laughed a little.

"You forgot how beautiful I am. When I opened that door, wearing that red teddy, you couldn't keep your hands off me or your dick in your pants." She smiled seductively.

"Not to mention your 8 stacks I had strapped to my body. That had ya big ass dick hard as hell!" She finished with laughter.

"Yeah, you sure looked sexy as hell in that teddy. But it was the paper that did it for me! That shit had my dick stupid dumb hard!" They both enjoyed some laughter. D-nice reached over to the nightstand, grabbed the half of a blunt and sparked it.

"Yeah, I know how that money be having you, but it can't make you nut like I can." Maliah said as she climbed on the bed.

Maliah had had been kissing all over D-nice for the last two minutes. He was buzzed from the clip he smoked, with the thoughts of how good Maliah's pussy was. Something she was trying to tell him last night popped into his head. During her kisses he stopped and asked her about it.

"About last night...what were you trying to say?"

She sat on him in a riding position.

"What I said to you last night is real, D"

"Refresh my memory and start from the beginning."

Ten minutes into Maliah's story, D-nice interrupted her.

"Aight, so let me get this straight. You might be pregnant, and you believe it's mine? The police brought you up here because your mother told them about G-money killing your brother, right?"

D-nice did not wait for an answer. He continued with his questions.

"So know yall in the Witness Protection Program? Check this out. For starters, here is two stacks for your troubles, abortion and whatever else. As for you, staying out here with your rat ass mother, that might be the best thing for you." He finished as he pushed her off him and began getting dressed.

"Please papi! Listen you're not getting it." Before she could finish, he cut her off.

"Maliah, you're not getting it! Look, I dig your style girl. But that shit you caught up in, is not something I keep in my circle. It's not my style shorty."

Maliah sat on her bed sobbing in tears.

"I know you and Games are close. And I also know that yall were close to Swift. When I realized G-money was fucking around with Swift's daughter, I knew I had to tell you."

"Tell me what?" D-nice was getting impatient.

"G-money and my brother are the ones who killed Swift."

"What the fuck did you just say?" he asked in shock.

"And how do you know all of this?"

She stood up on her feet and walked towards him.

"Nitty and my mother used to date. That is how my brother and G-money stated hustling for Nitty. It was Nitty's idea to get Swift out the way. He came up with a plan to get Swift out to BK, so my brother and G-money could rob and kill him. How do I know all of this? They planned the shit in my living room. After it was all said and done, G-money was bragging to them about how Swift tried reaching for his gun. And how G-money put two in his head before Swift could do so."

D-nice couldn't believe what he just heard. It sounded crazy ass hell, but it could all be true. The first thing he did was call Games."

---

GAMES SAT on the bench reading a newspaper in front of the building. He just finished off a clip from this morning and now he was a bit buzzed. So buzzed to the point he never heard his phone ringing. When the phone started ringing for the second time, Games picked up on the first ring.

"What is it like, Nice?" he asked.

"Yo skarp, we need to talk, like yesterday." D-nice replied.

"Aight, then spit it out, no Harlem." Games said with laughter.

"Ayo skarp, this shit is serious, not over the phone."

Games could hear the severity of the situation in his voice."

"So what you waiting on? I'm at the main location Nice."

"Aight then, give me an hour."

"An hour?" Games asked.

"Yeah Nigga, I'm at that location with shorty."

"Oh, you still out there? That pussy must be platinum, Nah, I'm just fucking with you. An hour it is. Don't take too long either, I got shit to do."

"Not after you hear this shit Skarp. It'll be the first thing on your to do list today."

"Well stop bumping your gums and get here then." Games said before hanging up.

---

AS SOON AS D-NICE LEFT, Maliah got on the phone. It rung three times before she got an answer.

"This Slime, speak." The caller answered.

"I know who I'm calling! And I'm sure you're wondering who I am. But that is not important. Just tell ya boy G-money, that his little secret is out. And within the next hour, I'm sure Swift's daughter will know too!"

Maliah hung up after she said what she had to say. She felt it was her job to make sure G-money's life be put to an end. Nothing would make her feel better than knowing she was the cause of it.

---

GAMES AND D-NICE smoked a blunt filled with sour, as D-nice ran everything down to him. They sat in D-nice's White on White 745i.

"I couldn't believe the shit when she told me." D-nice said as he took the blunt.

"Yeah, this shit crazy, way too crazy. I got to hit Rockie up right now." Games said as he pulled out his phone.

# CHAPTER 32

Zoe Stood on the curb, next to his truck while eating a big bag of Doritos. He was waiting on Rockie and G-money to come out of the doctor's office. Zoe's cell phone rang, and he knew it was Hots based on the ringtone. He wiped his cheese chip fingers on his pants then picked up.

"What's going on boss man?" he answered.

"Everything good my boy, what's up with yall?" Hots asked.

"Just waiting on them to come out the doctor's office. They should be coming out soon."

"Aight cool. I'm on my way to the private port now. Ty and the Mrs. Just pulled up. So we will meet up yall there. By the way, Rockie's truck is finished if she feels like picking it up." Hots explained.

"Copy boss man, I'll tell her the good news. Here they come now."

"Aight. We'll be waiting, One." Hots said then hung up.

Rockie and G-money walked out of the doctor's office and were all smiles. They had just learned, Rockie was carrying twin girls. Rockie was so excited that she cried. She could not hold her excitement in, so she called her mother first. After a few minutes of sharing the news with her mother, she called her twin. Of course Rah Rah cried when she shared the news.

"I'm so happy for you Rockie. And I cannot wait until my nieces get here. I'm going to spoil them rotten." Rah Rah whined as her eyes were filled with tears.

"I can imagine." Rockie replied as they made their way to Zoe's truck.

Zoe saw the happiness in the couple's face and could not wait to hear about it. G-money approached him and gave him dap and a brotherly hug. Rockie embraced Zoe as she was getting off the phone with Rah Rah.

Once they climbed into the truck, G-money had an idea to go see his mother. He wanted to see her and tell her the good news.

"Ayo Zoe, head out to my mother's crib really quick." He said. Rockie snapped her head in his direction.

"Glen, are you crazy? That's too dangerous."

"I know Rockie, but I have to see my mother and sister before I leave. I also want to tell her the good news in person.

"I don't think it's a good idea Glen." Rockie whined.

"She's right G, we shouldn't be riding around like this in the first place." Zoe added.

"Look, I'll call my mother and have her meet us on Queens Boulevard. Over by the McDonalds." He said pulling out his phone to call his mother.

Rockie understood his excitement but did not think it was a good idea. Against her better judgement, she told Zoe to follow G-money's instructions.

"Go ahead Zoe, but I think we should go somewhere closer. That way your mother does not have to come too far. And we have to make this quick."

"Aight." Zoe said in an unsure tone.

"I know the perfect spot." G-money said.

When G-money's mother picked up, he explained what he needed her to do. Without so much as a question, his mother did as

she was asked. They got dressed and snuck out through her backyard, into another backyard. Within the next five minutes, they
awaited G-money's arrival.

On the way to G-money's meeting spot, Rockie got a call from
Games.

"Damn Rockie, this like my third time hitting ya phone. Shit
really crazy, we have to get up like yesterday." Games said in a
frantic tone.

"Damn Games, slow down. You sound as we had a block party
or something."

"At this point, I wish it were a block party. But this cannot wait
to be addressed, so please get here quick."

"Alright, Alright....as soon as I'm done with dropping G-
money...."

"No!" Games cut her off.

"You might not want to do that after this. So please make that
U-turn and don't make it hot." He finished.

Rockie had cut her eyes at G-money then quickly looked
forward. G-money had been watching her since she answered the
phone and asked her. "Is everything aight baby?"

"Yeah, just something out in O.V. Aight Games, I'll hit you
when I'm on my way."

Before she could hang up, Games replied.

"Rockie don't hesitate, this shit has a lot to do with Poppa
Bear." Then the phone went dead.

Just as Rockie's phone call ended, Zoe was pulling into a driveway. The home they pulled up to was owned by a childhood friend
of G-moneys. Inside the house, G-money's mother and sister
waited for them. When the truck came to a halt, G-money asked
Rockie if she was coming in. From the mention of her father, all she
could do was stare at him. It was as if she did not hear him. All she
could do is think of the worst.

"My future, what's up with you? Is there something you need
to tell me?" G-money asked.

Rockie had a hard speaking. After a few seconds of silence, she came up with the quickest lie she could think of.

"Babe, I need to call my twin, it's important. Tell your mother, I'll come see her once I drop you off."

"You sure?"

"I'm sure. This must be attended to. Please go ahead and make it quick." She said touching his lap. G-money leaned over and kissed her on the lips.

"We will talk when I get back." He said then quickly got out of the truck. Once he closed the door, Zoe turned around and asked.

"What's going on boss lady?"

---

AS SOON AS G-money stepped into the house, his mother ran into his arms. She began asking question after question.

"Baby are you ok? How's Raquel? Is the baby ok?"

"Ma Relax! Just relax." He began while holding her shoulders.

"Everything is good ma. I'm just here to tell you Raquel is having twins!" He finished with excitement.

His mother blew put air with a sigh of relief.

"So why did some guy call me saying all this crazy stuff."

"What guy? And what stuff?"

G-money's mother began to explain the call he received from Slime, who did not leave a name. He did say that G-money was in very big danger, and it was important that he call him at a number he left. The caller made it clear that it was worse than the police looking for him. And that it was a life and death situation. G-money did not understand. After giving his little sister some love and talking for a few, he grabbed the number from his mother.

"Who dis?" he asked with a stern voice. He expected it to be Nitty but was surprised when Slime spoke.

"This your boy Slime, from Edgemere! First let me ask, is ya shorty close by?"

"Why?"

"Listen my boy, she shouldn't be hearing this conversation." G-money went to the window to pull the curtain back. Zoe's truck was parked, and he was sure Rockie and Zoe sat patiently waiting.

"Everything clear, so speak to me." He said to Slime.

"Aight! Check it, I got a call about 20 minutes ago from some broad." Slime began explaining the phone call he received from Maliah.

When slime finished explaining what just happened, G-money was stuck. He thought about the phone call Rockie received before they got there. He then asked Slime did he think she knew.

"If she don't know now, she'll get the call real soon. Shorty didn't sound like she was playing my boy."

"I'm going to need your help" G-money began.

---

ROCKIE SAT in the back of the truck with tears in her eyes. The mention of her father brought a pain to her stomach, more so her heart. Zoe could not get her to speak, so he called Games himself. He put his phone on speaker and listened to Games give him the run down.

"Are you sure about this Games?" he asked.

"It sounds about right. I got my team checking into everything, including Nitty."

Rockie spoke after hearing Games break everything down.

"I wanna holla at shorty face to face. Get on that Games. I'm about to call Hots and tell him about this. In the meantime Zoe, I need you to go inside and get Glen. Tell him we have to go now! If he don't rush out, then bring his ass out. I'm sure you know what I mean." Rockie spoke giving orders like a boss as best as she could. She had to stay calm under the conditions she was in. She climbed out the truck and leaned against the door staring at the house. Zoe tucked his 9mm Barretta under his shirt as he walked toward the house.

"Zoe was surprised to see G-money stepping out of the door as he approached.

"Took too long, my bad." G-money said stepping off the porch.

G-money seemed very happy to Zoe, but he could sense the nervousness when looking in his eyes. Before Zoe could reply, a white on white Charger pulled up right behind his truck. The sound of tires coming to a screeching halt, had Rockie's and Zoe's attention. Both watched two dudes hop out, one holding a Mac 11 in hand. Zoe told Rockie to get in the truck.

"I'm not going anywhere! Glen what the fuck it going on?"

"Well. For starters, please do not reach for your piece Zoe, or you will leave me with no choice. My future, I can explain. But you must be willing to listen. Put your emotions to the side."

"How the fuck could you say put my emotions to the side?"

She began walking towards him.

"You know some shit I don't?"

Slime interrupted with, "Ayo G-money, we can't sit here like this."

"Just chill Slime! Please Raquel, you got to believe me..."

Before G-money could finish his sentence, Slime's partner squeezed off multiple in his direction.

Rockie ran for cover towards the back of the truck, while Zoe pulled his gun returning shots.... BOOM!BOOM!BOOM!

G-money hit the ground in pain from the impact of the Mac 11. He quickly jumped up and started running toward the house, where his mother yelled and screamed for help. He made it inside safe as Zoe gave him cover.

Zoe shot his way back to the truck, where Rockie was safely cuddled in the back seat. He wasted no time starting the truck and pulling off.

"You good boss lady? Are you hurt?"

"I'm...I'm ok. We have to go back for Glen." She cried.

"We can't do that Boss Lady. Police will be all over the place in seconds. I have to get you home so we can figure this out safely."

Rockie cried in the back seat as she dialed Hots number. He picked up on the first ring and she could not have been more grateful . Rockie cried, sobbed, and stuttered while trying to explain the situation. The only thing Hots could tell her was to get home safely, and he would be there in an hour.

CHAPTER
33

R ockie listened to the news on every channel while confined
in her room. She felt embarrassed, defeated and like a failure. Rockie crawled up in a fetal position, drowning in tears. She
gave two orders and has not spoken since. The first was to make
sure she spoke with Maliah in person. The second was to get Hots
on the phone. Rockie had lost her cell phone while running from
death. Rockie felt there was nothing else to talk about. Not even
her mother was able to break her out of the bubble she was trapped
in. Rockie could not face her mother nor her sister. She knew her
father was looking down on her. With this in mind, she wanted to
fix this before speaking to anyone. Rocky already felt like a failure
them.

Rockie flipped through the channels on the T.V., trying to find
something else to watch. All channels spoke on Glen bring America's Most Wanted. Glen was involved in a shoot-out, that resulted
in the murder of a 17-year-old kid.

But it was no use though, Rockie was sick of it and cut the T.V.
off. She cried harder with her face in the pillow.

"How could you do this to my family?" She asked Glen
through sobs and tears. She wished he were able to hear her. Or

that anyone could. It was as if no one heard her cries. Not even her father. This caused her to cry some more and crawl up in pain. The babies were kicking a moving up a storm.

There were three soft taps at the door, causing Rockie to look up at it. She stared at the door knowing it could not be her mother or sister. They both banged for the first twenty minutes and came back within five, to bang some more.

Zoe thought it would be a good idea to allow Rockie some alone time, so it wasn't him. Games stayed close to Rah Rah and kept in touch with D-nice while he hollered at Maliah. So Games stayed cool and had nothing much to say.

The same three taps came again, but this time, a voice called out her name. For some reason, the voice brought her enough strength to get up and open the door.

Rockie saw the worry the eyes of Hots.

"It will be aight." He said softly.

She wanted to believe him. She needed some assurance or at least him to promise her it will be. She asked in a soft and weak tone.

"How could you be so sure of it?"

"Because I will not rest until I can see to it, that everything is aight. Believe that. Now we can talk." He finished.

It was the first time since the chaos that she even thought to smile. As bad as she wanted to, she held it in. She moved to the side to let him enter.

"So you don't wanna talk to ya family?" Hots asked as he entered. Rockie closed the door behind them.

"Do you even understand how I feel?" She said with an attitude.

"No, I don't! But I can tell you this, a boss is only a boss if he... or she, can make sure his team eat. A boss will be quick on their toes no matter the circumstance. Be ready to face anything at any time. And if need to, cry or mourn. But do it after you have celebrated your victory. And you do it with the ones you LOVE, ya feel me?"

"So far, I got Games and D-nice working on a meeting with Maliah. I need to speak to her face to face. Gle...G-money does not have much family, so he will run to a friend. I just have to find out, which one." She explained after soaking in Hots cologne, he was wearing Burberry Curve for men. Rockie could not help but be attracted to him. And if she wasn't before, she was now. Something about his energy and swag, gave her strength to fight her sorrow and pain.

"That's a big start. So how about I help with finding G-money? I mean, I got some niggas out here that'll shake Queens up." Hots said.

"Where don't you have people that'll shake up the place?" She asked, now allowing a small smile. Rockie had teary and puffy eyes, swollen cheeks and dry lips looking at Hots.

"A few places....but not too many." He replied with a sly grin.

"But seriously, I'll get them on that while you and I pay shorty a visit."

"Sounds good to me."

"Aight, now we talking."

Rockie went to wash her face. She changed into a pink and grey sweatsuit with a pair of grey, pink and white 95 Air Max, before heading downstairs. It was time to face her family. Rockie had her grey and pink Nautica bubble resting in between her arms, as she walked down the steps with a strong stare. Her mother was the first to grab her and speak.

"I love you Raquel! Are you ok?"

"I'll be ok. Are you good?"

"I'm fine baby. Just worried about you."

"Not to worry, would be a foolish thing to say. But I'm ok. I can assure you that. Twin come here. I'm so so so sorry." Rockie said to her sister. Rah Rah ran to embrace her twin and let some tears fall.

"It's ok twin, I promise it will be."

"Just be careful, remember...."

"I'm an auntie." They both said at the same time, with Rockie cutting in on what she knew Rah Rah would say.

After Rockie kissed both her mother and twin, she explained to everyone what she needed. Everyone had a job to do.

"Zoe, you and Games are to make sure that my mother and twin stay safe. Maybe even taking them to your spot in Long Island Games. This way, no one will be able to find them.

D-nice and Hots will go with me to talk to Maliah. Meanwhile, Games have ya boys spread out through Queens and find G-money. We have to find him before the cops do."

"Raquel, you cannot be out here like this! It isn't safe." Latasha said firmly.

"Ma, what are you talking about? I will not sit around waiting for Glen to get caught by the police to spend the rest of his life in prison. Or worse, be killed by someone else while trying to run and hide from the police."

"But it's dangerous Raquel! Now please stop trying to be your father for a minute. Take a step back and look at what you have to lose."

"That's just it ma! I can never stop being my father's child! And I have plenty to lose...but LOVE will run forever. Now can you please go with Games and Zoe? And take Rah Rah with you. I'll be ok!"

Latasha just sat and stared at Rockie. She could not believe what was happening. She knew her daughter's determination could not be stopped. She looked up at Hots, the look was of pity.

"PLEASE KEEP MY DAUGHTER SAFE." Was the look on her face.

Games nodded his head to let her know he understood.

"Aight family, lets get on our job." Hots said to everyone.

Latasha and Rah Rah stared from behind the curtains. They watched Rockie and Hots jump into his Benz and pull of with a truck behind.

HOTS PARKED his 2009 black on black CL65 AMG Benz, on Liberty street in Spring Valley, New York. Rockie sat in the passenger seat with a nervous look on her face. Hots had his top two goons, Ray Ray, and his man Flex, parked on the corner behind him. They sat in a black Cadillac Escalade with D-nice in the back seat. D-nice had just hung up his cell phone from talking to Maliah. D-nice told her that he and Rockie were outside waiting. Maliah rushed off the phone to get downstairs. He texted Rockie.

*"She's coming down now."*

"Don't look so nervous. Boss up, you can do this. We went over every angle there is. Just don't allow your emotions to get in the way of what's important." Hots explained to Rockie before allowing her to get out of the car.

"I'm ok, thank you." She replied reaching for the door.

Hots stopped her with a touch on her arm.

"If you need me to sit with you, I will."

"Thanks, but no thanks. You have done so much for me Hots. It's time to put my big girl pants on." She answered with a light smirk as she turned to open the car door and stepped out. Hots could sense her uneasiness but smiled back.

"She's so pretty and determined." He thought to himself.

Rockie stepped out of Hots' Benz and walked towards the truck. D-nice stepped out the back and held the door open for Rockie to get in. As this happened, Maliah made her way around the corner. She noticed D-nice before he noticed her.

"Hi Papi." She said walking up on him.

D-nice took notice of her disguise and shook his head with humor. It was both funny and cute staring at a tom boyish looking Maliah. She wore a Yankee fitted over her ponytail, loose sweatpants and an oversized Pelle Pelle leather. Maliah could have easily been mistaken for a Hispanic male teenager.

"What up Maliah? Rockie is inside waiting on you." He replied opening the door for her as he did Rockie.

Flex, who was sitting in the passenger seat, stood outside the truck while D-nice took his position. Just as D-nice took his seat, Rockie began. Rockie introduced herself to Maliah and explained why she needed to meet her in person.

In return, Maliah did the same. She went on to say....

"I won't waste your time Rockie. I'll start from the beginning and when you have a question, please feel free to ask."

Maliah began telling her story. She started with how her brother and G-money grew up as best friends and their connection to Nitty.

Nitty dated Maliah's mother and this is how they began dealing with him. Nitty would set people up from Brooklyn to Queens and have G-money and her brother as his gun boys. They also sold drugs for him as well.

It wasn't until Nitty felt his connect, which was Raquel's father Swift, was holding back from him. Nitty thought they were partners. Once Swift would not allow Nitty to meet the connect, or wasn't giving him any more weight, he decided to set him up.

Maliah then explained the day her brother and G-money were getting the run down from Nitty.

"And how do you know about all this?" Rockie asked.

"They were always in my house when they planned their attacks. And this day was not any different. They sat in the living room planning the attack on your father. I was in the kitchen, eavesdropping and being nosy."

Maliah finished the story with explaining that G-money was bragging about it. He made sure to let everyone know Swift was reaching for a gun, as G-money ran down on him.

Maliah left nothing out.

Including the attraction her and G-money had for one another since they were kids. And that neither of them acted out on it, out of fear of how her brother would take it. Maliah even told Rockie about the night of New Years Eve when G-money dropped her off.

Rockie stood strong after hearing all of this. At this point, she wished she invited Hots to sit in with her. After asking a few questions, Rockie asked the last and most important question of them all.

"What's your purpose for spilling all of this now?

"I'll be honest with you, it's because he killed my brother. The most important reason is my mother does not care about the rules of the street. She is gonna go all the way with taking the stand. Even if it kills her!"

This caused Maliah to choke up a little and she some tears as she finished. Before I let my mother go that far and basically get us both killed, I had rather put it all on the table. The truth! Then let it play out how it does."

With a phony smile, Rockie expressed her appreciation to Maliah. She took Maliah's number down, promising to call if her needed to. D-nice let Maliah out and promised he would call once he was done with his business.

The second Maliah was out of the truck, Rockie began crying. Once D-nice hopped back in, through sobs Rockie said to him.

"I...I want her and her mother dead."

"D-nice was caught by surprise by her bluntness but understood. He wondered if she knew about Maliah being pregnant by him.

"Do you need to ride with us or...?"

"Nah, I'm good. I'll see yall back in Queens." She said cutting him off as she got out the back seat.

As she made her way towards Hots' Benz, she called Games to tell him her plans. Once she hung up, she got in the car.

"Did you learn what you needed?" Hots asked.

"More than I can swallow."

"I see, you look like you been crying."

"Just a little, I'm ok now. I just want to find Glen. And I want that bitch and her rat ass mother dead!"

Hots listened to Rockie the entire ride back to Queens, and she was appreciative of it. He did not speak once, until they were sitting outside of her house.

"I told you before, and I'll tell you again, we're family and family takes care of each other. So whatever you need me to do, consider it done."

"I just need you to find Glen...Please!" She said through sobs.

She began to cry again when Hots started speaking.

"Give me 48 hours Raquel. I'll get that nigga!"

Before she even realized what, she was doing, Rockie had leaned over and began kissing hots.

# CHAPTER 34

L ater that night, Games sat in one of the spots he ran in O.V. He was talking to one of his people out of The Bronx.

"Yo Smurf, I need you to handle something...it's big!"

"You already brah! I'll be out there in like an hour tops."

"Aight brah, one." Games said then hung up.

Games stared at his most loyal goons. Ratley, D-nice and Dro, all started back at him. After a few silent minutes, Games expressed how dangerous this mission was. And how much everyone had to pay attention. Games told them about Kourtney being the driver. He called her up to come to the spot.

45 minutes later everyone was in attendance, including Game's man, Smurf, and Kourtney the driver.

"Good looking on these silencers Smurf, cuz we're gonna need them." Games said while looking at the 4 silencers laid on the table.

"That shit ain't about nothing. It's what we do" Smurf replied.

Games went over the plan once more while everyone was there. Blunts filled with Sour was being passed around while everyone listened thoroughly. In the middle of Game's speech, his cell phone rung.

"Excuse me people." He said then answered his phone.

"Talk about it"

"Yo Games, I got somebody you might wanna meet with." The caller said.

"Oh yeah? Well that shit must wait. I got some important B.I. to handle tonight."

"Aight, but I think Nitty is important B.I. that can't wait for later. From what I hear, he won't be around later."

"Where am I meeting you at?" Games asked.

The called has his full attention at the mention of Nitty.

"In the back of Edgemere at 12 tonight."

"That's a copy." Games replied then hung up.

Games turned to his people and told them there was a change of plans.

"Why what's good?" Dro asked.

"I just got a call about bigger fish. And I have to be there in two hours if I wanna catch that bitch. So Smurf, you in charge with Dro by ya side. I'll hit Little up to take my place. Any problem with that?"

"Yo to be honest, we don't need brah, we got this." Smurf said.

"You sure?" Games asked

"I'm positive! We got sharpshooters if need be. Now we do not have much time so let us get on it...and pass that sour. I need my medicine." Smurf said.

"Everyone laughed and Games passed Smurf the blunt.

---

KOURTNEY DROVE a blue Charger with Ratley, and Smurf ducked down in the backseat. She rode past a black Impala with three detectives' inside. Kourtney made her way around the block, driving to the back of the apartment building. After noticing nothing else out of the ordinary, besides the expected Impala, she said.

"Ok boys, yall on." She parked the car in the opposite direction for their perfect getaway.

Smurf took out his twin 40 Glocks with the silencers attached to them. He then grabbed the small Gucci bag that held two 9mm Berettas with the silencers attached as well.

"The Tech 9 and AR15 are in the small duffle bag for any surprises, ya dig?" Smurf said to Ratley.

"I'm good with the one in my lap and the other right by my side." Ratley replied as he began taking their guns out.

Smurf looked up and down the block before crossing the street and heading into the back of the building. As he entered the building, he placed his micro earpiece in and set his Swatch watch for 2 minutes. They all wore the same earpieces and watches.

"1st and 2nd base, I'm in. Time two minutes." He said as he pressed on his earpiece.

"Copy 3rd base, I'll be in less than two." D-nice said walking around the corner and into the apartment building. He carried a shopping bag filled with fruits. As he walked, he made sure he got a good look at the black Impala and the three heads inside. From what he could see, the detectives were having coffee and donuts.

"I'm in 3rd base, on my way up. It looks like the flies are comfortable on their shit." D-nice was referring to the cops.

When D-nice got to the 4th floor, Smurf was already waiting on him.

"You ready my nigga?" Smurf asked.

"As ready as I'll ever be." He replied while pulling the 9 Berettas from the shopping bag.

"Aight, but I think a quick prayer is good for the soul. Plus this is ya seed."

D-nice nodded his head in agreement. Smurf placed the nose of his guns on his forehead and D-nice followed his gesture.

"God please forgive us for the sins we're about to commit." Smurf said and they both said 'Amen'.

D-nice pressed the dial button on his cellphone. When Maliah answered he said.

"Surprise Mami, Papi is right outside ya door."

Maliah was so happy to hear his voice, she never hung up the phone. She rushed to the door and opened it without a second guess or thought. The second she had the door open and was staring at D-nice, she quickly regretted it. With his gun pointing directly at her stomach, she was unable so get a word out, let alone a scream. Before she could blink, two shots hit her in the stomach that sent her flying backwards into the apartment. Smurf rushed into the apartment jumping over Maliah's half dead body. He heard the scream of Maliah's mother.

"Maliah!" She yelled with a Spanish accent after hearing the loud thump of Maliah's body hitting the floor.

Smurf rushed to the back following the screams of the mother. As soon as she came rushing out the bedroom door, Smurf squeezed two shots into her head, silencing her for good.

D-nice had put another bullet into Maliah's head. Right after, a big "BOOM" shocked him. When he realized what had happened, he was halfway out the door, laying on his back in pain. An officer came out of a side room and quickly fired a shot from his 9mm. D-nice thanked god he had a vest on. Once the pain subsided a little, he began squeezing shots in the direction of the officer. The officer hid behind the bedroom door. Through his shots he could hear

"...the Titanic is sinking...I'm...I'm hit!"

"Where the fuck did he come from?" D-nice thought to himself as he pushed against the hallway wall.

"1st base waterfall, we need a home run." He repeated this before sending more shots through the door.

Smurf came running out the bedroom after hearing the loud shots from the officer. He was just in time to see the cop peek his head out for a good shot. Smurf took aim and squeezed two shots at the cop's head, hitting him once.

Ratley screamed through his earpiece.

"One got passed me! Only two down here, they MJD!"

(Michael Jackson Dead)

D-nice got up slow with the help of the wall. As he made his way to his feet, the third cop Ratley let get away, was at the top of the stairs. He had his 9 Glock pointing at D-nice. They both took their shots with the officer hitting D-nice in the neck. But not before D-nice landed a few into the cop's chest, sending him falling backwards down the steps.

"...Puh, Puh, Puh..." three shots from Smurf's 40 Glocks put an end to the cop who fell down the steps. He rushed back up the steps to D-nice. D-nice was bleeding out heavy from his neck and chocking on his own blood.

"Get up D, get up! I'm not gonna leave you here." Smurf said as he tried to pick D-nice up. He dragged him from under his arms into the house.

"2$^{nd}$ base get the fuck up here! 1$^{st}$ base...I need help!!!"

Just as he finished crying out for help, he heard sirens.

Ratley stepped into the apartment...

"Help me get him to the car." Smurf demanded.

"Let's go boys, their too close! We have to go now or we'll never make it." Kourtney yelled.

Through gags and globs of blood coming from his mouth and nose, D-nice managed to say.

"Go...get outta here" He coughed and choked as he tried to keep speaking.

"I, I won't make it...tell Games and Rockie...LOVE!"

Smurf was pissed at the fact they lost a true soldier on his watch. He wanted to kill Ratley right where he stood. But knew Games would be hurt by his drastic actions. Smurf laid D-nice's head down and said a quick prayer over him. Smurf and Ratley ran down the back steps and out the back door. Before walking out of the building they heard a loud shot.

"I guess he didn't wanna die at the hands of a cop." Smurf thought. Once they were in the car, Ratley took the wheel while

Smurf laid in the back seat. Kourtney rode shot gun as he drove on the back blocks and on to Liberty St. They got out just in time, there were multiple cop cars rushing to scene.

---

MEANWHILE IN BROOKLYN, Zoe, Games and two of Zoes's African comrades made their way into a building. Games received solid information Nitty would be there tonight.

Nitty was throwing a small stripper party for his B-day.

He had four strippers in the apartment with ten of his closest Brooklyn goons. There was plenty of bottles and smoke being passed around, as they threw stacks of money at the strippers. The four strippers were putting on some spectacular performances. There was nothing these women would not do for the love of them money.

Stripper #1 was pushing a Rosé bottle in and out of stripper#2 pussy. Meanwhile, stripper #3 was eating stripper #1 out as she was bent over in doggy style, putting in work with the Rosé bottle. They were going at it and nobody wanted to miss a second of it.

Bu Shakur was one of Zoe's comrades. He stood 5'8" weighing no more than 150 pounds but was truly a beast. Bu Shakur was one that had a sensational thrill for slicing throats, then licking the blood off his knife. He was 5 beers short of a 6 pack. He knocked on the door as if he were the police. In his right hand, a Rambo knife and in his left, a Tech 9 with a silencer attached.

When the 6'2", 220-pound, bald headed security guard opened the door, he almost laughed at the sight of Bu Shakur. He had no time to laugh as Bu Shakur pushed his knife right above the giants' dick. It was almost as if Bu Shakur was giving the giant a C-section. He pulled the knife out and went straight for the giants' throat. Slicing it with one swift motion.

The music was so loud nobody heard the giant hit the floor. Zoe, Games and Zulu came running into the apartment. The living room stood still when they realized Games and his goons were standing there. They guns pointed in every direction. Zoe help two AP-9's that carried 21 shots a piece.

Zulu had two P89's and Games held a Mac 11 with a silencer and an extended clip.

There was no need for talking, their guns would do that for them. They fired into the crowd, not caring who they hit. Everything moving got hit, leaving no one breathing.

Games recognized Nitty as Nitty tried running towards the back of the apartment. But Games was on him, like white on rice.

Two shots hit Nitty in his legs, sending him falling to his face. By now, everyone including the strippers, were laid down with multiple gunshots to their heads and body.

Games reached Nitty who was crawling on his stomach trying to escape the wrath. Games kicked him in the ass.

"Turn ya bitch ass over and face death." Games said.

Nitty turned over trying to beg for his life.

By now Zoe was standing right next to Games.

"We don't have much time Games"

"Listen this is not my fault." Nitty tried to explain.

"I guess you can explain that to the big homies Swift and Fresh when you see them. Let them know the family said LOVE"

Games and Zoe emptied their clips into his face and body.

As they were making their way out of the apartment, the saw Bu Shakur slicing the throats of each dead body. Zoe screamed in their native tongue.

"Let's go Bu, we have no time for that shit."

With that said they were on their way just as fast as they came, headed back to Queens.

---

ROCKIE LAID in her mother's bed while her mother sat rubbing her four-month belly.

"My grandbabies are moving." Latasha said happily.

Rockie just smiled.

She noticed how happy her mother was when she told her she was having twins. This made her think of G-money then her father.

"My will grow up fatherless, why?" she cried to herself.

"What's wrong baby? Latasha asked, feeling Rockie tense up.

"I guess I'm just thinking about the twins and how they're going to grow up without a father. Almost like me and Rah Rah." She said through light sobs.

"Don't you worry or stress yourself with that. Your father left you and your sister enough jewels to last three lifetimes over! We got this, ok?"

"I guess you're right."

"I know I'm right." Latasha said with a big smile.

"Thanks ma, you and dad are the best."

Rah Rah walked into the bedroom as Latasha and Rockie were hugging each other.

"Can I get some of all that?" Rah Rah asked with the same big smile Latasha just had her on her face. She walked up to the bed to join in on the love.

# CHAPTER 35

Hots was on his last set of push-ups. It was something he did every morning, and this morning was no different.

His cellphone rang just as he finished his last set. With his washcloth, he wiped the sweat from his face as he went to pick up his phone off the table. He watched as Rockie slightly moved on the couch. She was waking up from her deep sleep when Hots decided to let his phone go to voicemail.

"So the beauty finally awakes." He said with a light chuckle.

Rockie slowly adjusted her eyes to the sun beaming through the window. She stared up at Hots chiseled chest and found herself secretly lusting over him.

"Damn, I fell asleep on the couch?" She asked out loud but was more so questioning herself.

"Thanks for staying the night." She finished.

"It's nothing. Now get yourself up so you can wash up and eat breakfast... Oh, and you can wake everybody else up while ya at it."

"Breakfast? You cooked?" She asked surprisingly as she sat up on the couch.

"Yeah, a little something...I like to eat, Now hurry before the food gets cold. I have to check on some things, so I'll meet yall at the table." He said grabbing his cellphone and walking to the bathroom located in the back of the house.

Hots called his girl and soon to be baby mother back. She had been blowing up his cellphone since last night. He sat on the toilet waiting for her to pick up. She picked up on the second ring.

"Hi Shawn, where da fuck are you?" she asked with an attitude.

"Simone if you don't calm down with all that attitude."

"Or what? You didn't come home last night, and I'm not supposed to have an attitude?"

"I told you I'm in the middle of some real important shit."

Simone sucked her teeth then replied.

"I guess the middle of some stripper bitch legs is more important than ya family, huh?"

"Why you gotta be so stupid?"

"Oh, so I'm stupid now?"

"You talking stupid! I told you I am handling business, that's it! Now I'll be home in an hour or two." He said then hung up.

Hots could not take arguing with Simone, he loved her too much to do so. Hots knew arguing would only fuck up what they had. So he put his cellphone on ignore and dialed up his man GemStar.

GemStar was from Far Rock and ran half of Edgemere. Him and Hots met up north where they became close friends. They have put a lot of work together and considered themselves to be brothers. When GemStar answered on the third ring, he was happy to hear from his brother from another mother.

"What's popping bro, it's been a minute? What you been up to, and why such an early morning call?"

"So many questions at once, I don't think I have time to answer them all"

The two laughed a little, then Hots continued.

"Check it though, I need a trace on some nigga named

G-money from Red Fern. Maybe we can meet up and discuss the rest."

"I know son! And I just heard some shit. Aight, I will hit you in an hour for a meeting spot and we will chop it up then. One." GemStar hung up.

Hots did the same and began taking a bird bath. His phone rang again, and he checked to see who was calling. It was Egypt, the same girl Simone was referring to when she called. He met her a year ago in a strip club and was feeling her. But at this point, he did not have time for her. He let the phone go to voicemail.

---

ROCKIE HAD WOKEN up everyone for breakfast before she went to take a nice hot shower. While she showered, she could not help to think about G-money. She really loved him, and it hurt her to know that he had to die. The tears began to fall as she turned the water off. She got out the shower and went to her room to get dressed. She threw on some Juicy Couture sweatpants and a t-shirt. Rockie had not realized how long she had taken as she was slipping on her slippers and began to head downstairs. By the time she arrived in the kitchen, everyone was already seated at the table. Rockie did not know Games, Veronica, and her boyfriend Dro were attending. She smiled at everyone as Hots pulled out her chair to sit down.

Rockie look down at what was on the table. There were scrambled eggs, hash browns, grits, turkey bacon, pancakes, and sausage links.

"This is a feast! Why thank you sir." She said.

Everyone laughed and Hots just looked at her like 'Yeah right'.

"When did you have time to cook all of this?" She asked.

"I'm an early bird when it's time to get the worm."

"Well, now that we're all here, lets bow our heads and give thanks." Latasha said.

They bowed their heads and closed their eyes as she said a prayer. When she was done, they all said Amen and began eating.

"What's wrong Raquel? You're hardly eating. What, you not jacking my cooking?" Hots asked.

"No, I do! It's just, I don't know...I'm..."

Hots cut her off.

"Stop worrying yourself Raquel, it's not healthy for the babies. As a matter of fact, finish eating and then we'll discuss somethings."

"Aight."

When breakfast was done, Latasha, Rah Rah and Veronica cleaned the kitchen. Rockie sat in her father's chair in his office as Hots, Games and Dro stood around as Games explained what took place last night.

Rockie did not want to believe that D-nice died while on a mission, to kill a woman who was pregnant with his kid. Due to his loyalty to her and her family, she told Games she would pay for his funeral. Rockie also wanted to provide the family with whatever they needed.

"Whatever you want to happen, consider it done." Hots said.

She looked up at him and blushed a little.

Hots then told her about his phone call to GemStar and their meeting.

"I wanna go." She said.

"How about you relax until I get all the info needed to find this dude. It's just a meeting for information."

"Are you sure?"

"Always! I will take Games with me for a proper introduction to my man. It'll be good for future plans." Hots said looking in Games direction.

"That'll be cool." Games replied.

"Aight, but can we hurry up with this? Please?" Rockie asked but it sounded more like a demand.

"You got it girl! Let's get on with this." Hots said to Games. Games told Dro to hold down the crib just in case G-money showed up. And with that, Hots and Games left the house. Rockie went downstairs with Dro as they joined the other ladies.

---

G-MONEY SAT in the living room of his man Chubb's crib in the South Side of Queens. He could not believe he had made it out there after taking a shot to the chest.

After being shot, G-money ran into the house and out through the back. With his mother crying hysterically and trying to get him to go to the hospital, he knew he would have to get away from her. G-money knew at this point his mother had forgotten he was a wanted man. G-money had luck on his side, at least he thought so.

After running out the back door and making it two blocks up the street, his boy Chubbs happened to be driving by.

Chubbs stopped at the light and out of nowhere, G-money came from behind a parked car. G-money stumbled onto the front of Chubb's hood. When Chubbs noticed it was G-money, he got out and helped him into the back seat.

"Ayo G, what da fuck happen?"

"I, I'm shot." G-money said, barely able to speak.

"We gotta get you to a hospital."

"No! I can't go to no hospital."

Chubbs decided to go to his mother's house, with hopes that G-money made it. It took a few hours for Chubb's mother to pull the bullet out of G-moneys chest. She stopped the bleeding and made sure to stich him up good.

Once she was done, Chubbs took G-money to his crib, where he and his girl lived.

G-money was in a lot of pain and needed something for it.

"Yo Chubbs, I need some pain killers or something." He said in a low tone.

"Morena should be back any minute now. She went to pick up a few things from the store, so sit tight my nigga."

Chubbs said as he took a seat across from where G-money laid.

"So what happened my nigga?"

"Man, this nigga Slime tried to off me." G-money said.

"Word! But then again, I am not surprised. You know he fuck with that dude Nitty hard body. You know that nigga Nitty got 50 stacks on ya head."

G-money was not really surprised at what he was hearing, but pretended to be...

"Oh word! That snake ass nigga. I should've known not to trust no BK nigga." G-money said.

As he sat quiet for a second, he thought about Raquel and the safety of her and the twins.

"I gotta call my shorty. Let me use ya phone."

Chubbs passed him his burn out.

"That's a burn out. We gotta be careful. I'm holding a fugitive in my crib. You know you all over the T.V and shit." Chubbs said with a smirk.

G-money smirked a little then asked.

"Who said I wouldn't make history?" With an even bigger smile.

Just as Chubb's girlfriend Morena walked in with a few groceries, he was telling G-money he would leave him to his phone call.

G-money listened to the phone ring three times before it went to voicemail. He tried a second time and got an answer on the first ring...

"Hello?" Rockie asked in an annoyed tone.

He sat silent for a second which made Rockie ask again.

"Hello?!"

"Raquel...It's, It's me." Was all he could say.

"Where you at?" She asked in a demanding tone.

"I'm safe for now, but we need to talk. You have to believe me when I say, I didn't know."

"I will not talk to you over the phone. So tell me where you at and I'll come get you." She said cutting him off.

"Raquel, I'm not stupid. Now we can meet, but if you cannot meet me by yourself, then we will have to talk like this. I love you more than anything Raquel and I need you to understand..."

"Understand?" Rockie asked, now agitated.

"How the hell you want me to understand you taking my father from me?" She finished with tears coming down her face.

G-money knew she was now crying. He also heard a male voice in the background. He wanted to ask who the voice was coming from but knew better. G-money got back to her questions.

"I didn't know!" He screamed, which caused him a sharp pain in his chest.

He leaned over and asked Chubbs to bring him them pain killers.

"We'll since you didn't know, know this, you better hope the authorities find you before I do! You might be better off in jail Nigga!"

When the phone went dead, G-money was in more pain then before he got on the phone. That sounded like the Rockie he first met, and it did not sit right with him.

G-money knew the power she was connected to, and this made him think of his mother and little sister.

"I gotta get them safe." He thought to himself.

Chubbs walked into the living room passing two pills with a glass of apple juice.

"Yo G, take this and chill, cuz what I'm bout to tell you is gonna fuck you up." Chubbs said.

Chubbs sat down in his seat and told him about the phone call he just got. It was about Nitty. He left nothing out, making sure G-money understood the seriousness of the situation.

"Then on the news, it said that you got shorty and her moms hit, along with the police that was watching over them. Maaan, they making you out to be some Al Capone ass nigga. You getting all these people knocked off like that just put you on top of the list of America's Most Wanted. You're the most wanted since the niggas who brought down the Twin Towers down." Chubbs finished.

G-money could not believe all of what he was hearing. He thought about Maliah and her mom's being killed while under the witness protection system. Then Nitty and his whole team. "Damn Rockie." He thought to himself.

CHAPTER
36

R ockie, Rah Rah and VVS were sitting inside Swift's office
when Hots knocked on the door. Rockie was upset with
herself, she felt as if she had lost control when speaking to G-
money. She was caught off guard and allowed her emotions to
control her actions.

"Come in." Rah Rah said.

Hots walked in with the twin's mother.

"Baby are you ok?" Latasha asked as she walked toward Rockie
to hug her.

"I'm good, I guess."

"Don't worry about it Raquel. He can't get out of Queens
without being snatched up, So I'm sure he won't attempt." Hots
explained.

"But I lost control of the situation and might've blew our opportunity." She whined.

"Excuse me ladies, may I get a minute with Raquel alone?"
Hots asked.

Once the girls stepped out, Hots began explaining to her what
he had.

Hots man, GemStar, plugged him in with some young dude

from South Side named Murda Muzik. GemStar also told Hots how Nitty put 50 stacks on G-moneys head. That explained why Slime and his boy were there. Slime was supposed to pretend as if he were there to help G-money. When they got him in the car and away from the family, they were to kill him.

"So what is this Murda Muzik dude suppose to do?" She asked interrupting his explanation.

"Let's find out together." He said dialing a number and putting the phone on speaker.

The phone rung three times before anyone answered.

"Who's speaking?"

"This Hots, GemStar gave me ya number. Said you'll be expecting my call."

"Oh yeah, you just on time. I just got a location for that PK, so you wanna meet up?" Murda Muzik asked.

"Name the place and I'm there."

"109 and Guy Brewer."

"Aight, I'll be there in 30 minutes." Hots said then hung up. As soon as he hung up Rockie said.

"I'm coming."

"I wouldn't have it no other way. But you're riding with me."

"And I wouldn't have that any other way." She replied feeling the urge to kiss him. She stared up at him thinking of all the support he had been giving her and her family. Hots was also feeling the tension. He stared back at her but did not know what do or say. That was until Rockie stood up on her toes and planted her soft lips on his. All he could do was accept and embrace the kiss.

To the both of them, it felt right, but hots knew better.

He was glad when his phone rang, interrupting the dance between both their tongues. As he separated himself from the beautiful feeling, Rockie stepped back...

"Girlfriend?" she asked with disappointment in her tone.

"Let's get ready for B.I. Excuse me, but I need to take this." He said to her.

Rockie wanted nothing more than to handle business, so she walked out her father's office with her head held high. On the inside, her attraction and feelings for Hots was becoming harder and harder to deny. But with revenge on her mind, she knew she had to get her mind right. Rockie walked to her room to get dressed for the ride. While she was getting dressed, she explained to the girls what was about to take place.

Hots lead the way with Rockie riding shot gun. Behind him was Games and Dro and behind them was Hots goons, Ray Ray, and Sleep. They rode three cars deep through Queens and Rockie could not have felt more confident.

The sun already went down, and the night life had begun. When they pulled up on the corner of 109$^{th}$ street and Guy Brewer, it was packed.

"Why would he tell you meet him in such a crowded place?" Rockie asked staring out the window on to the crowded corner.

"I was thinking the same thing, but hood niggas do hood shit. And he is keeping himself safe, so it is understandable. A bit sloppy, but understandable." Hots answered.

"Too sloppy for my liking...you got an extra gun?"

Hots laughed a little then replied.

"I promise you're good, just relax and trust me."

Hots then threw the car in park and jumped out.

With Games and Dro standing outside their car, along with Ray Ray and Sleep right behind Hots, the situation was under control. Rockie sat in the car staring at the people on the corner.

Hots and Murda Muzik dapped each other up.

"What's up with that paper?" Murda Muzik asked after their dap.

"That's not an issue, but ole boy is." Hots replied.

Murda Muzik smirked.

"I see! I watch T.V and shit. I tell you what, step over here with me." He said walking away from the crowd.

They stepped off to the side after Hots told his goons to sit tight. They were only a few feet away. And after a sip of his drink, Murda Muzik said.

"This is the deal, I got the address to where son is. The only thing about it is, it's my sister's crib. She's the one that put me on. Her boyfriend fucks with son and calls himself helping the nigga out. So all I ask is that my sister stays safe. Not a scratch. Once I get that paper I am supposed to get, this'll all be over."

"Are you coming?" Hots asked.

Murda Muzik looked at him and thought.

"That's all this nigga is going to say".

But out loud he said

"I can follow."

"Then let's go." Hots said as he turned to walk away.

"You lead the way." He finished as he kept stepping.

---

G-MONEY WOKE UP FEELING TRAPPED. He was sweating and in a lot of pain. He sat up and looked around the living room. It was a bad dream he had that shook him up.

He grabbed the pain killers that rested on the table. After taking two pills, he washed it down with a bottle of water.

He noticed Chubbs girlfriend standing in the kitchen doing the dishes. What she wore had him staring longer then he intended too. The boy shorts she had on had most of her ass cheeks fighting to be released. The small snug t-shirt and thin waist made the sight all the better to look at.

G-money was caught off guard when Morena turned around and asked.

"Does this sight make you feel better?"

He could not find the appropriate words to say. She smiled with a sly grin then asked.

"Are you hungry?"

"Nah, I'm good. Where's Chubbs?" he asked, now confused.

"Asleep upstairs. Why, do you need him?"

"I'd appreciate it." He answered.

G-money needed to get out of the house. His mid was on a mission that he had to put into action. G-money watched a Morena walked up the steps and thought.

"Under different circumstances, I might've taken the bait."

He got up and walked to the mini bar to pour himself a shot of Hennessey.

"I need this." He said out loud, but in a whispering tone. He threw the shot back then poured a second one.

"That might not be good for you and ya condition." Morena said as she made her way back downstairs.

"That's just it, this is needed under these conditions." He replied, a bit startled by her reappearing so fast.

"I hear ya. Well your boy said he'll be down after he finish feeding the sharks."

He laughed at the terminology she used to describe Chubbs taking a shit and she laughed with him.

G-money made his way back to the couch and sat down. Morena went back into the kitchen to finish what she was doing. But this time, he could see the mirrors plastered over the stove. He watched as she worked around the kitchen. G-money was sure she knew he was staring because of the way she maneuvered around. She bent over more than he believed she had to. And swayed her hips harder than necessary. Morena even looked back a few times to make sure he was watching.

When Chubbs came walking down the steps, G-money did not hear him due to Morena's performance in the kitchen. That was until Chubbs spoke.

"Rena, I told ya ass to stop walking around the house like that when we have company."

"Oh please nigga, this my mutha fucking house. Don't like it? The door is open." She shot back.

G-money knew at that point who ran shit around the house. It was obvious that girl was too much for Chubbs.

"It has to be his paper that keeps her around." He thought. He watched as Chubbs just waved her off, sucked his teeth and then walked into the living room.

"The mouth on bitches today is reckless, but I ain't tripping. That same mouth is great for a lot of other things." Chubbs said with laughter.

G-money joined in on the laugh then dapped him up.

"What's good my nigga? I see ya feeling a little better." Chubbs asked as he took a seat across from G-money.

"Yeah, a little something. That brings me to my next favor...I know you got a burner, and I need to hold ya car."

"Damn my nigga, the car? I just got that thing."

"Listen, if need be, I got enough paper at mom dukes' crib. I am sure I'll be bringing ya joint back in one piece. I just need to shoot out to Bay Waters really quick."

"Aight, I got'cha. I got this 9mm Taurus for ya, brand new out the box. The keys are on the key ring by the door."

"Good looking my nigga."

"I know I'm good looking. You just be careful my nigga." Chubbs replied with a grin on his face.

---

HOTS PULLED up on the opposite side of the street the house was located on. Him and Rockie watched as Murda Muzik pulled into the driveway of the house. Murda Muzik directly parked behinds Chubbs 2008 Lexus LS 300. He got out and looked up and down the block. He then looked across the street at Hots and nodded his head as he walked to the front door.

Hots hit Ray Ray on his phone and told him to be on point.

Ray Ray and Sleep were parked around back just in case G-money tried escaping that way.

"We here my boy, up and ready." Ray Ray replied as him and Sleep stood outside of his black 2008 Yukon Denali.

Hots got out his Benz and told Rockie to stay in the car, as he made his way to the front door to meet Murda Muzik.

Just as Hots and Murda Muzik were about to knock on the door, it opened. Hots quickly raised his gun and pushed Chubbs back into the house. Murda Muzik followed behind him with his 357 Magnum.

"Don't even think about no crazy shit." Hots said punching Chubbs to the floor and pointing the gun in G-moneys direction.

G-money looked at Hots then Murda Muzik, then back at Hots. He was staring Hots down hard. G-money wanted to reach for the new 9 Taurus that rested on his waist.

"Come on son, don't make this shit harder than it already is." Murda Muzik said as he inched closer. G-money slowly backed up as the pain in his chest began to ache.

Rockie sat patiently, but her patience had run out after seeing Hots go in with his gun drawn. After a minute passed and there were no shots, she decided to go see what was taking them so long.

She got out the car, walked across the street and up to the door. She thought to knock but thought against it.

"Why should I? Hots is already in there." Rockie turned the knob and stepped in.

When G-money saw Rockie step into the house, causing Hots and Murda Muzik to take their eyes off him, he took that second to throw his body into Murda Muzik....

"BOOM!!!"

# EPILOGUE

5 months later, Rockie laid in a hospital bed giving birth to her twins. She was in labor for two hours when the first baby came out, weighing 7 pounds 1 ounce.

Rockie was crying, screaming, and yelling for the doctors to get the second baby out. Sweat fell from her face as she closed her eyes as tight as she could and pushed harder.

"Please, Please...come out." She yelled out of breath to her child. The pain was so unbearable that she lost consciousness for a couple of minutes.

---

"OH SHIT!" Hots yelled as he dove to cover Rockie from the shot that went off. But he was too late. Rockie fell backwards from the impact of the bullet. Still, Hots was able to fall over.

Meanwhile Murda Muzik and G-money tussled and rolled around the floor for control of the gun. The second shot went off and G-money was able to get up and run toward the back of the house. Before he took off, he paused to see Hots holding Rockie in his hands. Blood was visible and G-money wanted to run over there to help, but he knew it would cost him his life.

Chubbs screamed for G-money to come on, as he ran toward the back of the house.

Hots ran after G-money once Rockie assured him that she was ok. When he passed the kitchen, he saw Morena was ducking behind some cabinets. He quickly stared but kept running. Ray Ray and Sleep heard the first shot and pulled their guns from their waist and rushed to the backyard. By the time they reached the door, G-money and Chubbs were coming out. Ray Ray and Sleep drew their guns, pointing them directly at G-money and Chubbs.

"Where da fuck yall think yall going?" Ray Ray asked.

G-money and Chubbs stopped in their tracks. At that moment, G-money wished he had pulled the gun from his waist. Now he was a sitting duck.

Sleep walked up in G-money and hit him over the head with the handle of his 9mm Desert Eagle. G-money's legs quickly gave out from under him as he fell to the floor unconscious.

"Put that nigga in the truck, and don't forget to tie him up." Ray Ray said as he pushed Chubbs back into the house.

"Where's G-money?" Hots asked.

"Sleep got the nigga in the truck."

"Aight, leave this nigga. He don't got nothing to do with this. We out! I gotta get Rockie into my car, she got hit." Hots said as he rushed back to Rockie.

When Hots reached Rockie, she was up on her feet leaning against the door. She watched as Morena tried consoling her brother.

"You good my nigga?" Hots asked Murda Muzik as he walked pass him and his sister.

"I'm good...I think."

"Aight, well you could easily say niggas tried to rob yall. The paper in ya car...we got what we came for. Come on Rock." He said to Rockie as he wrapped his arm around her waist and led her out the door.

Inside Hots car, driving at 50mph, he made his first call to a close friend.

"J-lo I need you like yesterday." He said to the person he called.

"What's going on? I'm in my office."

"Need a doctor fast!"

"Amy stay at my old condo in Manhattan. I'll call her and tell her you're on your way."

"Thanks J-lo. I'll hit you up later." He said then hung up.

As he dialed Ray Ray's number, Rockie asked who was J-lo. He stood quiet as if he didn't want to answer...

"Girlfriend huh?" she asked now feeling drowsy and in a lot of pain. Hots was happy Ray Ray picked up.

"Dro take that PK to the point."

"Copy, Copy! You good?

"I will be... I'll get back to you in 30." He said hanging up.

"Is Glen aight?" Rockie asked.

"Don't know how long that'll last though." He replied.

"I, I need to see him...alive."

"You will, but for now we have to get you to a doctor. So why don't you just relax, because you're losing a lot of blood being so hyped up and shit."

Rockie felt a sense of jealousy, but the pain was becoming too much to deal with. Not to mention she found it hard to stay up. And as began dozing off, she thought about G-money. She hated him for putting her in her current situation. Her babies would feel it more than anyone, which made her want to kill him herself.

In two days Rockie had a plan. She had a sore shoulder from a bullet that went straight through. Hots had her medicated and sewed up in Queens resting. Rockie was more than ready to see G-money. It was all she thought and dreamed about for the past two days.

Latasha and Rah Rah were not taking no for an answer when

Rockie got up and announced that today was the day. At first, she did not want them to have any parts of it, but quickly realized they deserved it just as much as she did. Rockie called Zoe to pick up her mother and sister, and she would ride with Hots. She made sure she dressed the part, wearing all black.

She wore a pair of black stretchy jeans, a Dior blouse with 3-inch heels and a black Burberry pea coat. Completing her attire were a pair of Gucci leather gloves and black Gucci shades.

"I guess you are ready for this." Hots said as he took in her beauty and her attire.

"Not completely, but I'm sure you got that part for me." She replied as she took her seat in his car. Hots closed the door behind her and chuckled to himself.

The ride was quiet and intense. But once they were in Hunts Point in the Bronx, Rockie began to feel an anger arise and could not wait to get there.

Looking at the building from the outside, Rockie would have thought they were entering a nice hotel that was placed in the middle of the hood. Once inside, she learned that this building was just as abandoned as every other building on that block. Most apartments on the ground floor were door-less. The floor and walls needed heavy construction.

"Watch yall step." Hots said leading the way.

"You would've never thought it looked like this from the outside." Rah Rah said, stepping over some broken wood.

She held hands with her twin as they made their way up some steps.

Once on the second floor, unlike the ground floor, there were doors on the five apartments. Hots stepped in front of the last apartment door on the right.

"Are yall ready for this?" he asked the girls.

Latasha and Rah Rah nodded their heads, but Rockie asked.

"Is he in there?"

"He sure is."

"I need to see him alone first." She said.

"Are you sure?" Her mother asked coming closer to her and giving her a hug.

"Of course I'm sure ma. I need to do this, so give me a minute. Please."

Latasha stepped to the side as Rockie walked toward the door. Hots opened the door and peeked inside to tell his two goons to step out. When they did, he stepped to the side for Rockie to step in.

Rockie could not believe how G-money looked. Her heart, for that split second ached for him. He was beat badly. One of his eyes were tightly closed and swollen. His face was badly bruised, and his clothes were torn. She stood in shock for a second, but as soon as G-money tried to speak, her mind went to how her father was no longer with her.

"Don't! You have no right to speak." She said interrupting his cry of apologies.

Her heels tapped hard against the wooden floor as she walked closer to him.

Rockie stood directly in front of the chair he was handcuffed to and said.

"Do you realize my children will grow up without their father? They'll be just like me and my twin, the only difference with them, they'll never get to meet their father." Tears slowly began to form in her eyes

"You...you have to know I didn't know Raquel." G-money mumbled through swollen lips and missing teeth.

"Shut up...just shut up! You are a poor excuse. Remember me, my twin, and my mother, love our father and husband... L.O.V.E.! Loyalty Over Values Everything, and you, you have none of that. Within that word lies honesty and truth, along with plenty of more values. But you seem to not have any of these or carry them. So try to look at my mother and twin in the eyes with that one eye you got... I'm done." She then screamed out to Hots.

Hots quickly opened the door and Latasha and Rah Rah walked in first. He stepped in behind them.

Latasha was the first to speak.

"Glen, I can't believe I thought you might be the one for my daughter. All I need to know is why?"

"I'm, I'm sorry Mrs. Williams...I really didn't know." Glen replied.

Rah Rah walked back to the door and stood there with her hands over her eyes as the tears poured.

Latasha ran to her aid and now they both were caught up in their cries.

Hearing G-money not deny killing Swift, was a heavy blow to both Latasha and Rah Rah. And at this point, Rockie wanted him dead.

"Ma, Rah Rah, leave the room...Hots give me your gun." She said.

Latasha and Rah Rah were both hesitant, but Rockie gave them a look they had only seen on Swift's face. Latasha and Rah Rah reluctantly obliged.

Hots walked up to Rockie, passing her a 380 Glock with a silencer attached.

"Are you sure you wanna do this?" He asked.

Rockie took the gun without words.

She turned to G-money who was a couple of feet away.

"Tell my father why you're there. For once, be honest and hope he can forgive you. But tell him Rockie couldn't, L.O.V.E. is what he embedded in me."

Rockie took aim and fired the gun. She kept squeezing until there were no more bullets to shoot. Her tears fell as she dropped the gun in front of her. Hots walked behind her to console her.

Glen's body was hit from the chest up and Rockie never shot a gun before. As she stood to her knees looking down at a slumped Glen, she did not know how to feel. And then the pains in her stomach happened. The twins began kicking and stabbing her insides.

———

THE DOCTOR'S placed an IV into Rockie's arm and a mask over her face. For two minutes Rockie's body went weak and she was not conscious.

They made Latasha step out of the room, while they worked on Rockie. Within the next two minutes, Rockie was conscious again. However, in the process, they had to cut the little girl out of her and got her to breathe.

When Rockie was stable enough, the doctor's allowed Latasha back into the room. They placed the twin babies in Rockie's arms and she began to cry. After the doctor explained the procedures, Rockie named her daughter Hope and her son Loyalty. And she could not wait to tell Hots.

———

ROCKIE PASSED her business in the streets to Games, who just proposed to Rah Rah. He purchased a house in Long Island and a house in Atlanta. Once the twins graduated, Rah Rah would be attending Spellman College and he wanted her to be comfortable. Business was great on the streets for Games and he thanked Rockie, Hots and Ty every chance he had. Games went even harder to support Rah Rah on becoming a psychiatrist.

Between Rockie and Dro going hard in the streets with Games, VVS purchased a Barbershop/Beauty Salon. Her and Dro were one of the two youngest couples to own such a big place on Jamaica Avenue. It had twenty barber seats on the ground floor and upstairs had twenty beautician chairs. The place was set up nice thanks to VVS and Rah Rah's decorating skills. There were two flat screens, both 72 inches on each floor with surround sound. Downstairs looked like you walked into Madison Square Garden with top grade wooden floors set up like basketball courts. Upstairs was decorated with pink and lavender leather sofa's all around with flowers and roses all around the place. She name it 'VVS Palace' and was happy because all types of stars and celebrities came to her place.

Rockie set Zoe up so he could open his own cab service, out in Rochester, N.Y. He named it 'Nice and Smooth'. Zoe had all types of different cars and truck to call on.

———————

TY CAME to visit Rockie while she was still in the hospital. They were not able to leave yet because of Hope having to be monitored.

"How's Hope doing?" he asked as he passed her some flowers and gave her a hug.

"She's doing better. The doctor said we'll be able to take her home tomorrow."

"That's great."

"So how's Hots doing?" Rockie asked curiously.

"He's good. They gave him 3 flat, so he'll be aight."

"I heard he was out there in the BX being Larry Davis and shit, shooting out with police" she said.

They both shared a laugh.

"Yeah, he could be a bit crazy. Anyhow, he told me to tell you to take care of those twins like he know you will. He also...." Ty paused.

"What?" Rockie asked, looking him square in the eyes.

"Well, he didn't take it there with you because of the love he had for you. Not to mention, he loves the mother of his son. But he was already going through it with another girl, who might be pregnant. So he didn't want you caught up like that. He wanted you to know if he didn't have so much on his plate, he might've asked you to be his wife."

Those words brought tears to her eyes. Just the fact that Hots had enough respect to not take advantage of her, made her weaker for him. When she looked up, she was in Ty's arms.

"It's alright Raquel. On a happier note, congrats on the twins and those nursing classes at N.Y.U."

"Thanks Ty." She said wiping her tears away.

"So how's the NBA life?"

"Can't complain, just gotta get New York a chip before it's too late."

"I know that's right, well you got some big fans and heavy supporters."

"Thanks! Aight, let me get out of here. Gotta get home to the wife and jr."

"Alright Ty. Tell Ebony I said hello and give that young twin of yours a kiss for me. I almost forgot, tell Hots I love him and to keep his head up. And that I will gladly accept his proposal whenever it comes. That is if it don't work out where he's at." She finished with a smile.

The next day, Rockie left the hospital with Hope. Her mother and VVS came to pick her up. Rah Rah and Games had Loyalty at home with them.

Rockie sat in the back with the baby while VVS rode shotgun and her mother drove. They were having a light discussion about all their businesses without waking up the baby. Rockie's phone beeped to let her know she had a message. It was from a private line, so she rushed to check it.

"Congrats Indian baby." The message began and she knew it was Hots.

She listened intensely but not before telling her mother and VVS to be quiet.

"...happy to hear the twins are ok. Mainly Hope. I know she will be as tough as her mother. And Loyalty the same. He got Loyal to play with too. They will both be double trouble. Ha Ha Ha... Anyway, I hope your not too upset with me and overstand my position and what I am caught up in. You are a young woman that deserves so much more. So please accept my apologies and continue to stay strong. I will be in touch as long as I got Games to check for. L.O.V.E. my Indian baby. And just remember, I had to play my cards right."

After listening to the message she hoped things did not work out with him and his son's mother.

"How wrong is that? My Bad!" She thought to herself. But it's how she felt.

No matter what, to her Hots would always hold a place in her heart.

"And I didn't even get to sex his fine ass." She said to herself as she laughed out loud. At the end of it all, she said a quick prayer to God and her father.

"Thanks Dad, LOVE" She said ending her prayer.


**STAY TUNED FOR PLAY YOUR CARDS RIGHT**

One Year Later

The day Summer graduated from Park West High School, was a day she would not forget. Diamond rented out the 2012 Rolls-Royce Phantom. Everybody did stretch limo's and Summer wanted to be different, so she settled for the white Phantom. Her surprise was when Roach popped up out of nowhere. He walked in just as she was called to get her diploma. This brought tears to her eyes. Nanna, Diamond, Winter, Loyal and her uncle Chris were amongst the crowd. Uncle Ty could not make it because the Knicks made the playoffs, so he was away playing ball. Although he couldn't make it, he sent her a check for $20,000. She called Ty, Ebony and lil' Ty thanking them.

That weekend Roach took her and Isyss to Summer Jam and New Roc City. They had all the fun she could ask for, besides having her mother and father there to share the moment with. Now at 17 and out of High School, Summer wanted to get out and explore the world. Hots and Simone had her college bound ready and she promised she would not let them down. However, she felt as if she needed a year to spend some time with Roach, and to start working on designing for the clothing line she wanted.

Diamond hooked everything up with some people in that lane. Summer already had underclothes and two-piece bikini's selling out of stores. She was happy for it but knew she could do better. One of her short-term goals were to start shopping around some new sketches. She wanted to showcase these blouses and dresses she had been putting together.

In the meantime, she found her way to Miami with Roach for the week. They were on the beach enjoying the sand when she finally told him about the conversation she had with her father. "You're not serious, are you?" He asked in disbelief.

"So you're indirectly calling me a liar?" She asked while laying on her towel in one of her own designer bikinis.

"Why would I call you a liar? I'm just surprised. I know...well, I thought I knew Hots. And the Hots I thought I knew would not be liking this shit."

"Well he's my father and loves me very much. So he wants to see me with the best. And everything around me must be the best... and loyal too." She said.

"You know I know!"

"Yep, and he said you were the most loyal on his team. Out of all the people he knows you best and explained how you were like him, a player. He also said, he knew where home was. And if you are anything like my father, then you are all the man I want and need. Just know, when you decide to make a commitment to me, your player cards will be revoked."

"To be honest, if ya pops gave me the green light to be with you, then there won't be no playing ever again. I can't afford to be hunted down by your father or his crazy ass cousin."

They both laughed at the mention of Hots cousin, Murdok.

"So I guess that will make it official?" She asked.

"How can I decline being with someone as beautiful and smart as you?" He replied.

Summer jumped on him with so much happiness. They rolled over into the hot sand and began kissing passionately.

Summer was on top, so she was fine. But Roach could feel the hot sand burning his back. He did everything to fight it because Summer's kisses were that more effective.

After the beach they were headed to Roach's hotel room. As they walked down Sunset Boulevard, Roach squeezed Summer's hand.

"Ray, what's wrong?"

"Just keep walking and look toward the stores...ok stop." He commanded.

"What happened Ray?"

"You see that girl in the yellow? That's Melinda."

Summer could not see her face because the girl had already walked pass her.

"Are you sure Ray?" she asked.

"I'm positive. She cut her long hair to that Cassi style, but it is her. Now this is what I want you to do. Go back to the room and get my gun from out my Gucci bag. Once you come out the hotel call me, and I will lead you to me. I can't let her out of my sight." Roach explained.

Summer asked no questions, she just turned around and rushed to the hotel.

Summer was trying to find her way back to Roach. After getting her hands on the Glock 40, her urge to pull the trigger came back instantly. It was the first time she touched a gun since that day. And now, she was feeling it all over again. The gun rested inside her Louis Vuitton bag while she followed Roach's instructions and directions.

"Summer, I'm across the street from the Louis Vuitton store. There is a hotel right there. Just come inside when you get here." Roach said as he stepped to the man behind the desk. Summer was lost for a few minutes before she found the hotel within 5.

When she walked into the hotel, Roach was there to greet her.

"Let us grab a seat at the bar and I'ma get the gun. I want you to..."

"I'm going up with you." She said cutting him off.

"Don't do this Summer."

"That's my father and mother she put in jail. And I want to be there to see that she is dealt with. Now let's go, we're wasting time." She said walking to the elevator.

Roach just caught up with her, hating that she had to be there.

"How did you get the key to her room anyway?" She asked on their way upstairs.

"A Thousand and he doesn't know anything." Roach said with a smile.

"When we get in this room Ray, I'm sorry, but I have to put a bullet in that bitch's head."

"No." He said. Just as the elevator stopped and the doors opened, she stepped out. Roach grabbed her arm.

"Summer don't do this...I got it!"

"I know you do, but I want this one." She said as she pulled away. She stopped by the door waiting for Roach to open it.

"Here we go, do not hesitate to squeeze if it looks crazy." He said.

"Don't you worry about that."

When the door opened, Melinda was walking naked to the bathroom. She heard the door opened and turned around.

"Who's yall...Roach!" She said in a fearful tone.

"It's not him you have to worry about." Summer said raising the gun and pointing it at Melinda.

"Wait, wait, please I'm sorry. Don't do this, I got money!"

"Will that money get my father out of jail?" Summer asked.

Roach just stood there watching the ladies.

"Your father? You're Summer?"

"A Hots one too."

BOOM, BOOM, BOOM.

Summer shot Melinda three times, each one hitting its mark. Once she was down, Summer hit her in the head.

"Alright Summer, we gotta go!"

When they were downstairs Summer had a thought. She told Roach if they were to leave the hotel right now, they would be on camera.

"And the police definitely check the cameras." She said.

She suggested they get a room and give the man another band to stay cool.

"We can't trust that." She said.

"If you let me handle it, trust." Roach replied.

The hotel room cost them $3,000, not including the first band Roach gave him. It did not matter because around 12 midnight, they were leaving the hotel Scott free. Roach was more impressed with Summer, now more than ever. She got the man in the hotel to take the gun with no gloves on and then took it back.

"I'd rather take my chances. She said as if she changed her mind.

When they got back to their hotel, Roach ran some water and allowed her to soak in the tub. Summer appreciated how he always treated her. Not once did he ever try to make a move on her. After soaking and thinking to herself, Summer wanted to lose her virginity tonight. She got up out the tub and walked out the bathroom ass naked. Roach was smoking a blunt and drinking some Henny out a glass. His eyes opened wide as he just started with his mouth to the floor.

Her 34B-24-38 frame was immaculate in Roach's eyes. Her nipples stood at attention and was a milky chocolate color. Along with her light brown skin complexion, she was perfect in his eyes.

"I don't want to wait any longer. Have me Ray." She said walking toward him.

She left nothing for him to say and no room to breathe.

Within seconds they were kissing like they were used to doing it. But now, it would go beyond kissing.

. . .

WHEN SUMMER GOT BACK to New York, Murdok came to get her from the airport. Murdock was Hots cousin from Buffalo, NY. He was here to help Diamond with Hots business, plus he needed to get out of town for a while.

Summer liked him because he was cool and funny.

"So did you have fun kiddo?" He asked as he drove the Bentley Azure.

"Yep, but I'll doubt she'll be telling on anybody else." Summer said with much confidence.

"Sounds like you are your father's daughter."

"I'm a Hots Summer and a Cold Winter....but Hottie will do for now." Summers attitude went from 0 to 60 in just a few days. Only she knew what her next move was. She smiled as she thought about some things to herself.

Her phone had a text message that read.

"How long? Ya father wants to talk to you." She put the phone down.

"Daddy, it's on now." She said to herself.

"Murdok call Diamond!"

The phone in the back of the Maybach rung twice before Diamond answered.

"Summer Hi, how was your trip?" She asked.

"It was cool. How's everything on your end?"

"Fab-tastic If I have to say so. You sound a bit refreshed...Do I hear a...?"

"Murdok is listening and you're on speaker Diamond. But anyway, I'ma have him bring me by the shop. We have to talk." Summer said interrupting her.

"I'm not paying you two no mind, yall must've not heard this Weezy." Murdok said while listening and nodding to a track off Lil' Wayne's 'Dedication pt3' Mixtape.

"Anyway, yall come through because I have some news for you

too. Oh, ya father want to see you next week and you got a letter from ya mother the other day...by the way, I didn't know I worked for you." The girls let out a laugh and ended the call after Summer and Murdok said their goodbyes.

Summer dialed her house number and spoke to Nanna, Loyal and Winter. She told Nanna she would be home after the she stopped to speak to Diamond at the shop. She spoke to Loyal for a moment, his bad ass was too busy playing shoot 'em up games on the PS3. Talking to Winter was like talking to an older sister. Winter asked all types of questions down to who she was with, and when she was coming home.

"I'll be there tonight, and we will talk. I got to go." Summer said then hung up. "That little girl, she's only eleven!"

Her and Murdok laughed. Summer started thinking about Diamond and whether she should tell her about losing her virginity to Roach. She had already spilled the beans to Isyss the next day.

"What's on your mind?" Murdok asked.

"Nothing...just thinking about Diamond and what she has to talk about."

"More than likely, she got some good news, don't she always?"

"Yeah, she does. Murdok, let me ask you something..."

"Shoot."

"Do you think Diamond and my father were seeing each other?"

Murdok did not know how to answer that, but he was sure Hots was fucking Diamond cuz they spoke about it before.

"Ah..."

"You don't have to lie to me Murdok, I'm a big girl and I love my father regardless. It won't change anything." She explained.

"Yeah, aight little lady. Yes, he was seeing her. He took her out the strip club and gave her a job at the car shop. But I do not believe it was serious, he loves your mother to death."

"Spare me the extra shit Murdok."

"Watch ya tone little lady. I'm big bro regardless." He said with a smile.

"Well I'm Hottie and I'm the new boss of my father's business."

"Aight, you got that part, but remember, I'm still big bro!"

They continued to laugh and talk mess to each other until Murdok pulled up in front of the shop.

Summer stepped out the car ready to have the most enticing conversation with Diamond she would ever have with anybody. In her mind she was the boss already. And after what happened in Miami, it was no doubt that she was destined to be the boss of what belonged to her father.

Summer really like Diamond. She was only 25 years old, so Summer looked up to her like the big sister she never had. She really hoped Diamond would understand, because she would hate it if she had to remove her permanently. Summer also knew the visit with her father would be that much more interesting, but she had to go for it.

Roach was down for her and so was Murdok. Now all she needed was for Diamond to agree.

Summer was growing fast and had her mind made up. She made a promise to herself, that Winter and Loyal, will be forever good as long as she lived. She planned to open her own clothing store with the own clothing line. And a modeling business to go with it.

"Yall just watch how HOTTIE do it!!!"


BE ON THE LOOKOUT FOR...
"SUMMER'S HOTTIE BUT WINTER'S COLDNESS"
Coming soon!

Made in the USA
Middletown, DE
18 September 2021